I0623946

TAKE A MIND TRIP

TRIP

BOOK A FANTASY

Anthology of Award-winning Short Stories

Copyright ©2018 by Scribes Valley Publishing Company. All rights reserved. Individual authors in this anthology retain copyright to their material and all rights revert to them. No part of this publication may be reproduced, stored in a retrieval system or transmitted in any form or by any means electronic, mechanical, photocopying, recording, or otherwise, except in the case of brief quotations embodied in critical articles or reviews, without the prior written permission of the publisher and individual author.

The stories in this anthology are works of fiction. Characters, names, places, and incidents are products of the authors' imagination or are used fictitiously.

ISBN-10: 0-9851833-8-1
ISBN-13: 978-0-9851833-8-7

DEDICATION

This anthology is dedicated to those who
know what a mind trip is

To the authors featured in this book: Scribes Valley thanks you for
your time, patience, trust, and talent.

CONTENTS

Mind Trips – A Forward by the Editor   7

Caught – Catharine Leggett   9

In Vera Veritas – Ronna L. Edelstein   25

140 Over 90 – Bill Mesce, Jr.   37

Wunner If Elvis Got the Gun Instead? – Mike Tuohy   45

Joys – Lucy Marcus   51

Rules – Rebecca Evans   65

Lap Dance – Jennifer Companik   69

Punishment – Ruth Moors D'Eredita   81

Summer Memories – Dorothy Robey   93

Drenched – Israela Margalit   99

A Boy in the Woods – Carl Wooton   111

She Who Made the Land Her Home – Stephen Matlock   125

MIND TRIPS
A Foreword by David L. Repsher, editor

Trips require a couple of things. First, you have to possess a body. There is no compromise on this.

Secondly, trips require some form of transportation, and demand that you go by air, water, or ground. And, unless you are walking, you're surrounded by a human-made contraption that limits your space as you move to your destination.

A Mind Trip, however, is completely different. With a mind trip, you are limited only by your imagination. Wait...shame on me for using the word *limited*. I know better than that!

A mind trip is limitless and borderless. *Infinite* doesn't begin to describe it. It astonishes the human mind and ignores the laws of physics. In fact, it ignores every other law ever created, or ever will be created.

Luckily, you don't have to rely on my pitiful attempts at describing a mind trip. The stories in this anthology will show you exactly what a mind trip is—and how easy it is to take one. All you have to do is read the first word, and you're off.

Bon voyage!

FIRST PLACE

CAUGHT

©2018 by Catharine Leggett

Audrey met most of her close neighbors at the new condo before she officially moved in, when she dropped by to take measurements for window treatments and to meet a painter. Ruth lived next door, by herself. A divorcee, she wasn't one to mince words. "I would have preferred widowed, like you," she told Audrey. "I wanted to kill my ex so many times. He was such a jerk. Too bad it took me so long to figure it out. I'm never getting married again; I'm so done with that!"

On the other side, the Bennetts made it clear they were churchgoers, an initial offering of information loaded with underlying intent. They wanted to hear she went to church too, which, she imagined, would have them assume she didn't drink, smoke cigarettes or weed, or have late-night parties and long-term visitors. Audrey nodded and said, "I see." She didn't oppose religion, if people kept their beliefs to themselves. And that included New Age. Some wouldn't call it intolerance, but she liked to keep personal matters private.

Audrey had a list of issues she preferred to keep quiet: what she paid for her condo, her pension, what she did with her time, her age, though what good would it do anyone knowing she was 68? Or when David died. That one she choked on, barely able to say *two years*. Could it be? It seemed so long ago, and yet such a short while ago. When people chiseled away at her, poked and prodded for answers, she pretended not to understand or hear. Let them think she was standoffish, or hard of hearing. Suited her fine.

As the painter's van backed out of her driveway, a woman in a pink and blue floral maxi dress crossed the street and, with a broad smile, accentuated by pink lipstick, introduced herself as Mona. She asked for the particulars of Audrey's moving date, and if Audrey thought she'd love it here, and soon into their chat announced, "I'm a widow. I was happy to hear another widow was moving in. We need to stick together. Don't get me wrong. I was happily married for 38 years. But I'm quite capable of living on my own and I am very good at it."

As Mona talked, she faced Audrey's one-story, garden-style condo, identical to her own, except for the bistro table and chairs in her front patio enclosure. "There was a couple here before," she said, as if speaking to their ghosts. "They were so involved with themselves, so busy, they'd no time for anyone else. Not mixers. Isn't that why we move here? To mix?" Mona told Audrey she'd love living here and once she was moved in, they'd have to get together for tea. "Or maybe even something stronger, if you know what I mean." She gave Audrey a wink. Audrey did not wink back.

On moving day, while Audrey's movers were unloading, someone called from the open door, "It's me, Mona. I'm coming in." Suddenly there she was, a plate of cookies raised on the pedestal of her five fingers, making her introduction to Audrey's two sons and daughter. "Just a little something to keep the energy up." Her eyes cast about the open-concept kitchen, dining and living room area, the identical configuration of her own place. "Oh dear," she said as she took in the volume of boxes and furniture strewn about. "You're going to have to get rid of some of this. You've got too much stuff." She placed a hand on Audrey's shoulder and gave it a reassuring squeeze. "Don't worry, sweetheart, we all make the same mistake. It's hard to part with things, isn't it? Trust me, you'll get better at it." On her way out the door she called out, "You're going to love it here."

Audrey felt something go through her, a sudden dizziness, and rocked back on her heels. Perhaps the heat and the exertion of moving. If David were here, he'd insist that she take a rest before tackling more unpacking. If David were here, they'd exchange glances and get back to work, knowing that they would share their first impressions of Mona, their new neighbor, at the end of the day, over wine.

Finally, after several more hours of heaving, hauling, unpacking and sorting, Audrey declared the workday over, and time to order in. As they sprawled on the furniture they managed to clear, eating pizza and drinking beer, the front door opened and a voice carried down the hall. "Hello? Can I come in? It's just me, Mona, your new neighbor." For the second time today, there she was, standing in the great room in front of Kyle, Amy and Joey, clutching a large bundle of toilet paper. "I forgot to bring this over with the cookies. Oh, I see you're having dinner. Pizza's a good idea on moving night, isn't it? Something simple. Who wants to cook?"

Mona looked like she might be headed out somewhere, with her dark hair styled, not a hair out of place, her makeup fresh, her small feet elaborately wrapped in sandals with fake blue jewels, her hemline ending just above the knees. "There's a really good pizza place here in the neighborhood. Is that where yours is from?" Mona leaned over Kyle for a closer look at the slice hovering at his mouth. "That looks delicious, but the neighborhood place is much better and uses way more cheese. You'll love it!"

Kyle held the slice suspended in front of his mouth. He never liked anyone coming between him and his food, nor, for that matter, did he like meeting new people, not even as an adult, and especially not Audrey's friends.

Mona asked him how he liked his SUV. "I saw you get out of it in the visitor's lot."

"Company car," he answered, his articulation barely beyond a grunt. "Uses too much gas."

"Well, it's a good-looking vehicle, don't you think?" Mona appeared taken aback by his indifference, his utter lack of enthusiasm.

"If you like that sort of thing." Kyle placed his pizza slice on his plate, rose from his chair, and went out on the back deck.

Mona had to be off but wouldn't hear of Audrey seeing her to the door, though Audrey hadn't moved so much as a muscle in that direction, she was so tired. On her way down the hall she called out, "Once you're settled, we must get together. Don't leave it too long."

Lovely, fine, yes. Once she was settled. That would take a while.

On the way to the community mailbox, someone called from behind. "Audrey, Audrey, hello." She waited in the street for Mona to catch up to her.

"Hello newest friend," Mona said, her face alight with smiles. "I saw you headed out and thought I'd join you. Hope you don't mind. It's such a lovely evening."

Audrey explained that she was on her way to get the mail, for the first time.

"Feel like going for a walk?" Mona asked.

"I hadn't planned on it," Audrey said. She'd even been tempted to leave the mail for another day. A week after moving in, she was still working her way through boxes and every night collapsed into a spent heap. "I'm very tired."

"Oh, but it's such a nice night for a walk," Mona said. "It would do you good to get away from your work. Take a break. I see your lights burning at all hours. I find that it's just so much easier to give in to laziness then to get some exercise, isn't it?"

"I've been working all day, all week. I wouldn't call myself lazy."

"I didn't mean to imply that you were lazy. I meant *me*. But a leisurely walk is very different from being cooped up inside. A little stroll through the neighborhood might help you relax."

Did she need to relax? Was that the vibe she gave off? Well, what harm would a walk do, and maybe a change of scene would perk her up. Mona was right. She'd been working hard to get herself settled in, the way she went at everything. If David were here, he'd pour her a glass of wine and order her to sit down, but in his kindly way, accompanied always by a grin and a gentle chiding. *It's a good thing I am here to remind you when to quit.* And it was a beautiful evening, cooling down now with the sun setting. If David were here, they'd still be at the old house, and on such a night as this, they'd sit out on the back deck and talk.

As they walked, Mona filled her in on some of the people in the other condos: they both work; she is a divorcee, not friendly; the people in 36 don't pick up after their dog; the woman in 28 thinks visitors' parking is for her extra vehicles; those people broke condo rules and planted purple flowers instead of yellow; a lovely man lives in 12 and walks every single day, never misses; and the woman and her daughter next to him have tea on their front patio but never invite Mona to join them.

"You seem to know everyone," Audrey said.

"I was one of the first to move here," Mona said. "I *do* know everyone." This seemed to be a matter of some pride. "If there's something you need to know, just ask me."

Hearing about the new neighbors made Audrey feel lost, or perhaps a little depressed. But how could she feel lost in a city she'd lived in for so long? She'd only changed neighborhoods. She knew everyone on her old street where she'd lived for twenty-six years, and they'd settled into an unspoken, but consensual agreement about how they were with each other. Days, weeks, months would pass without her seeing anyone, until warm weather drew them out to the sidewalk to chat and catch up. Summers spent waving from the front porch. Shouts of hello as they took the garbage to the curb. Brief exchanges. And yet, after David was diagnosed, and for the weeks of treatment that followed, there they would be at her front door, delivering a casserole and offers to help.

She didn't want Mona to tell her about anyone else. It made her feel as if she didn't belong, that she was a newcomer, insignificant somehow, or worse, an interloper. As if she'd shed her past life and her identity along with it. Did she have to prove herself all over again? Being old in a new place didn't mean uninitiated.

She took hold of the conversation. "I like the little sitting area in the complex." Audrey pointed to the gazebo and the rose garden surrounding it, which abutted a large park. She'd noticed these features while condo searching, and it was the gazebo, the rose garden, and the park that finally sold her on the place. She'd only had a chance to visit the gazebo twice, but once she was mostly settled, she looked forward to sitting to admire the roses, take in their glorious scent, under the maple's shade. Of course, the gazebo provided its own shade, and a comfortable place to sit, a good resting spot on the shortcut to the park. No need to drive all the way around to the park's entrance. "There is nothing quite so exquisite as the scent of roses," Audrey said, aware of the whimsy in her voice.

"Oh, those roses," Mona said. "Let me tell you about that rose garden. It was supposed to be called a Peace Garden, but it's turned into a War Garden. I was against it from the start. Don't get me wrong, it looks lovely, but it must have people from our community working on it to keep it that way. Our landscapers won't do it; it's outside their contract. I wrote up a work calendar for sharing the weeding and watering, but people didn't turn up for their allotted times. I used to step in and do it for them, but no more. I've instructed the condo board to remove the roses and replace them with shrubs. See why? See those thistles? See how high they are? It doesn't take much for property values to drop. I am also pressuring them to get after the city to put up a fence between the park and our property. For safety reasons."

"I didn't notice the thistles," Audrey said, and stopped in the road. "I'm turning back. I'm tired."

Mona said, "This isn't where I turn back. It's up there, not far."

"I'm turning back now," Audrey said.

Sometimes Audrey drove to her old house and stopped out

front, peering under the covered porch with its two solid pillars, into the living room and dining room windows, as if trying to glimpse her past. She asked herself if she'd ever lived there, her old life so disconnected from her present it resided in her like a faint ache. Was she having an out-of-body experience, as if she'd jumped on board some shifting alternate universe? Even her old furniture didn't seem familiar, felt out of sync with the new place. The condo let in a flood of light that revealed the nicks and flaws, years of being bashed about by family life, hidden by the dark interior of her old house. She could almost see David sitting in his favorite porch chair, his tall lean body draped into it as easily as cloth, grinning as he stared out to the street, the ruffle of wind in the trees igniting his mind, his thoughts, his ideas. His imagination knew no limits.

Audrey squatted on a little stool in her patch of front yard, listened to the birds, inhaled the fragrance of turned earth and clipped grass, as she pulled weeds, a chore she performed purely for pleasure.

"Well, hello there, stranger," someone said from behind. "You don't have to do that, you know."

Audrey squinted up at Mona, standing before her in a smart summer shift and straw hat, a silk scarf draped around her neck, her lips painted a pastel shade. "Isn't that why we moved here, so we wouldn't have to do this kind of thing? Now put that sputter down and come with me to my place. Let's have a glass of wine! I haven't seen you for a while. I won't hear no!"

Audrey was not opposed to a glass of wine or two. She and David often sat out in the evenings, their favorite time of day, and polished off a bottle. The way Mona said it made it sound illicit, naughty.

Seated on Mona's deck, accompanied by the trickle of a water feature, surrounded by garden decorations, and after they caught up with regular chit chat, Mona said, "Do you mind if I am one hundred percent honest with you?"

The question startled Audrey; she wanted to say both yes and no. Something warned her she might not want to hear, since statements starting with such a leading question rarely took you to a place you wanted to go. If she said yes, she did mind, she'd always wonder what Mona was going to say. "No," she said. "I don't mind."

Mona refilled their wine before going on to her moment of truth, and settled into her wicker. "I tell it like it is and if people have a problem with that, they have a problem with me. What you see is what you get," she said, and Audrey could tell by the flames in Mona's cheeks the wine had kicked in. "If you don't like how I am, I'm sorry, because I'm not going to change."

Audrey felt dislocated again, as if she couldn't catch the thread of the conversation. Wasn't Mona excusing herself for anything she might say that could be offensive? Maybe it was the wine; it was late afternoon and she'd eaten very lightly so far today. She had a mild buzzing in her ears. Mona should get on with it.

"Well, if you don't mind me saying so," Mona said, "and if you don't mind me being blunt, that color of green really doesn't look good on you. It doesn't work with your skin tones. The style's nice, but you're more suited to beiges or blues. It's fighting your complexion, makes you look a little orange, if you want to know the truth."

Did she want to know the truth? The truth according to Mona? Audrey looked down at her tunic. Amy gave it to her two years ago for Mother's Day, shortly after David died. "Oh, really?" It was her most comfortable top. She wore it a lot. Probably because Amy gave it to her, and she liked the feel of the fabric against her skin; it breathed, didn't feel too restrictive. She would keep on wearing it.

Mona's justification for her fashion sense, she went on to say, came after years of owning her own dress shop on Princess Street. "The Gilded Plum. Do you know it?"

Audrey had heard of it, but never shopped there since the clothing was more elaborate than anything she'd ever wear.

"It was quite famous," Mona continued. "I had clients from all over the area, some from far away, who came to me for advice. They trusted me to choose their wardrobes. There were newspaper articles about me. My fashion sense is just a natural ability I have. Something I was born with. So, I hope you don't mind my comments about your top." Mona studied her for a moment then said, "Wait! I've got a good idea." She put her wine glass down and brought her hands together, as if capturing the idea between her cupped hands. "Let's the two of us go shopping and I could help you pick out some things. It would be fun! We could make a day of it, do lunch!"

Audrey hadn't given any thought to clothes since retiring, and even when she worked she paid little attention to fashion. It wasn't unusual for an academic to be more interested in comfort, but she'd always been like that. "Maybe," she said. "But I don't need new clothes right now. In fact, I need to get rid of some."

Mona made regular appearances at Audrey's. Suddenly, there she'd be at the door, borrowing a casserole dish, a cake pan, lawn chairs for an event she planned with distant relatives who were coming to stay. She brought Audrey an illegal weed killer for her front yard so she wouldn't have to dig them out, wouldn't hear Audrey's protests that she preferred not to use chemicals and enjoyed removing the intruders by hand, as well as the fresh air.

Mona pointed out ants in Audrey's driveway and warned her they'd get inside. She noticed Audrey put garbage bags out before seven p.m., the official time, and neighbors would report her to the condo board. Not her, of course not, she didn't mind, but others would. She loaned her an expensive air diffuser to rid Audrey's house of a lingering odor she detected from the previous owners. She loaned her a runner rug to protect the wood floors in Audrey's hallway, until Audrey got her own. Audrey didn't want to borrow any of these things, and she'd no intention of buying rugs, but Mona was deaf to *no thank you*. "Just a neighbor helping a neighbor," she said. "It's just how I am. Generous, I like to think."

Once, after Audrey declined her invitation to a fashion show, she said, "You keep too much to yourself. You should mingle more with people in the neighborhood. Remember, I warned you I'm honest."

Audrey considered herself social, but not with her new neighbors, and on her own terms. She met with old colleagues for lunch, belonged to a monthly book club and a knitting club, took aqua-fit classes, went out with a walking group, attended talks at the university, and took in plays and concerts. She accepted invitations from couples she and David used to socialize with when they both worked at the university, and who didn't sever ties when he died. She went to Toronto with girlfriends.

Mona said she saw the flicker of Audrey's TV sometimes when she got up in the night to go to the bathroom. "What are you doing up until 3 or 4 a.m.? Have you tried warm milk for sleeping? Once it's warmed, an ingredient is activated that helps you settle. Or make yourself something to eat. Porridge or toast. Carbs make me sleepy." Mona said she wondered sometimes if she should knock on Audrey's door in the night to make sure everything was okay.

Audrey had blackout blinds installed in her den, the room facing Mona's place. If she couldn't sleep, she didn't want it to be anyone's concern if she was watching TV, and she didn't want to be held accountable for it either, not even to her kids. Not that they ever asked how she was sleeping. She kept the blinds drawn in her great room and bedroom, just in case.

She started slipping out her back door so Mona wouldn't see her go for evening walks. She listened to pod casts on her cell phone, sat at the gazebo and smelled the tea-scented roses, took in the sky and the hefty sweeps of the maple branches. She crossed into the park and wandered under the ancient trees, strolled across the broad open field. While the weather held, this was how she treated herself.

One night, on her evening walk, she discovered the roses were gone. Dug up and removed from all around the gazebo, replaced by bushes that smelled like cat urine and would never look any different than the way they looked right now. Behind the gazebo, there was a new fence between the condo property and the park. A barrier, an obstruction. Nothing to admire while sitting in the gazebo, no fragrant breezes to inhale, and her beloved walking place cordoned off, the short cut to the park no longer accessible.

Her eyes stung with tears. Surely this wasn't a matter to cry about, but she couldn't seem to help it.

Mona approached her along the road. Audrey managed to say something about the roses and the fence. Mona didn't seem to notice her faltering voice.

"Yes, we finally got the roses out of there," Mona said. "No more thistles to contend with! The fence will keep undesirable people from the park out of our community. That should be reassuring to you, Audrey. It is for me. You just don't know who's in the park after dark. You can't tell me you didn't worry about intruders. Maybe you'll sleep better now."

Audrey became accustomed to the lack of light in her condo and holed up in her den. The back deck provided a daytime escape into light and air and away from Mona's prying eyes, and at night she used the front door, left the light off, and pulled her black hoody up over her head, merging with the shadows on the way to the gazebo where she sat listening to the restless sift of wind in the leaves. Before going back, she stopped at the fence to stare into the park.

She ignored the knocks on the door, knowing it was Mona, until Mona stopped knocking and Audrey hid in peace.

One autumn night, unable to sleep, Audrey pulled her black hoody over her pajamas and strode to the gazebo. She never went to the gazebo so late, but the idea of it energized her somehow, as if she were doing something illegal.

Wind whirled around her, whipped up memories of David. How

she missed him. The excitement of their conversations that lead to unexpected, thrilling ideas. His passion for science and his inventive mind took them beyond the restrictions of the present to the future, and made them hopeful, even though they both knew they'd be long gone, unable to witness if any of his predictions came true. It was what she missed most, she came to realize. The brilliant mind that knew no boundaries of imagination or impossibilities. The strutting off into regions unknown.

Her breath traced itself on the chilled air; her feet stained the dewy grass as she made her way to the fence. She longed to wander in the park, beneath the trees, and savor the luxury of being the only one there. She hooked her fingers through the diamonds of the wire mesh, then the tips of her shoes, and began to climb. She reached the top, swung her leg over to the other side, picked her way down most of it, let go, and dropped down into the park. She smiled all the time she walked, knowing that she was the only soul among the trees and under the lamplight, as if she were in a Magritte painting, a lone figure in austere light.

Her middle-of-the-night ramblings, cravings she could not resist, grew longer, and sometimes she returned to her condo minutes before first light touched the sky. She had to be careful or someone would see her, report her. News would fly around the complex. Neighbors would come to see her on the pretense of a social visit, but they would be there to assess her state of mind, see if she was *all there*, see if they should alert the relatives.

Audrey saw very few people at the condo, though she kept up her friendships outside of the complex. Winter set in, and she established a routine without her forays to the gazebo and park, whiling away her time with crosswords and reading, working on her tapestries, socializing with friends who didn't go south. She kept her tapestry work in the great room, worked on it when she felt the urge, and allowed it to take over the space, never worrying about putting it away for company. Her children were used to her messes. What they weren't used to was how she kept her blinds closed all the time. "Mom, don't you want some light?" they'd ask. She told them she felt like neighbors were watching her, and she didn't like it. They didn't push her, but she noticed their sideways glances, their way of registering that she might be losing it.

Audrey hadn't seen Mona in weeks, maybe months, but she never forgot about her completely. The blind in the den stayed down, lest she risk sending a signal that she was open for visits. Sometimes she wondered if her sense of privacy and independence had reached an unhealthy level, but she was happy not to suffer through unbidden opinions, superfluous advice, and spontaneous visits.

In the spring, Audrey resumed her gazebo sessions, and once again began climbing the fence into the park, looking forward to it in the way a high-jumper might anticipate breaking a record. The fact she could still do it gave her unexplainable pleasure, even elation. She could almost hear David saying, *You never cease to surprise me. Just one of the things I love about you.* Somehow, the secretiveness of her park escapes made them more exhilarating.

One warm night, after sitting at the gazebo listening to a podcast, she went to the fence to do her usual climb, and near the top, caught her pajama leg on a barb. She straddled both sides, balanced on the point of one shoe stuck into the diamond mesh. She could not break free and the wire at the top of the fence cut into her hands. She wriggled and jiggled her leg, but the fabric held, and after five more minutes of struggle her heartbeat became erratic. Could she be having a heart attack? Is this how her life would end? Stuck straddling a fence like an escapee?

Sweat poured down her brow but, balanced as she was on her hands, she could not wipe the drops away, and the salt stung. Should she call out, see if any of the other condo people could hear her? Or would they mistake her for some lonely creature howling in the night?

She let go and let herself fall toward the condo side. Her caught leg trailed and the wire spikes along the top of the fence gouged the inside of her thigh. Her cotton pajama pants ripped with the pull of her body against it, and for seconds she dangled upside down until the fabric gave and she dropped to the ground, stripped free of her pajama bottoms.

Audrey limped back to her condo, her leg badly cut, trickling blood and paining, her bottom bare for all to see.

It was Mona's fault. It was her idea to get rid of the roses and put up a fence. Audrey wouldn't be forced to go to such lengths, outrageous lengths, to have some privacy and enjoyment, if she could just be left alone, allowed to go about her day to day without—well what was it? An interrogation, an accounting of herself! Restrictions! At her age, didn't she deserve some freedom? The right *not* to have to explain?

Audrey stopped climbing the fence. She had to. Her leg, badly bruised, the scrape from the fence still red and raw. She could have broken something, of course she could have. A hip for instance. And what then? Off to the nursing home!

Sometimes, while sitting in the gazebo, she gazed down the fence where a shred from her pajama bottoms dangled like a flag. Caught in the act.

A knock came at the door. Against better judgment, she answered it.

It was Mona, holding something beautifully packaged and tied off with a pink bow. It was a candle, Audrey saw as Mona raised it up to her. Mona was all done up with coral-colored lipstick, mascara, her face a glowing bronze, her dark-brown hair professionally styled, a strand of lumpy orange beads cast around her neck. "I hope I am not disturbing you," she started. "I thought I saw a light on and I wanted to drop this off and tell you I am back."

"Back?" Audrey said. "From where?"

"South," Mona said. "I've been away for four months. Didn't the Bennetts tell you? They've been watching my place. I came to say goodbye, several times actually, but I couldn't seem to catch you at home. I brought you this. Just a little something to brighten your day. Cheery light. And it has a lovely scent. Like roses, since I remembered how much you like them."

Audrey stepped back, the wound on her leg sharply describing her movement, reminding her of her antics, her extremism. She reached for the parcel Mona offered and tears dribbled down her face. "Sorry," she managed.

Mona seemed stricken, caught off-guard. "It's just a little something, sweetheart. Really, nothing much at all. Nothing to cry about. But I'm touched. I really am. I'd never guess such a little gesture would mean so much to you."

Audrey heard David's voice. *You expected her to understand?* If he had been here, they would have laughed about the rose-scented candle, understood its far-reaching implications, and Mona's gesture would have been explained away as an ill-conceived good intention, nothing more. If he'd been here, there'd be no tears, no need for the dark. If he had been here.

About the author:

Catharine Leggett's short stories have appeared in the anthologies *The Reading Place*, *Slow the Pace*, *Lose Yourself* (Scribes Valley), *The Empty Nest* (KY Story), *Law & Disorder* (Main Street Rag), Best New Writing 2014 (Hopewell), as well as in the journals *Room*, *Event*, *The New Quarterly*, *Canadian Author*, and *The Antigonish Review*. Other stories have appeared online in *paperbytes*, *Per Contra*, and a novel excerpt in *Margin: Exploring Modern Magical Realism*, and broadcast on CBC Radio. A two-time finalist in the Columbus Creative Cooperative Great Novel Contest, her novel, *The Way to Go Home*, is forthcoming from Urban Farmhouse Press. A collection of short stories, *In Progress*, won the Eludia Award and will be published by Sowilo Press, an imprint of Hidden River Publishing, in 2018. She lives in London, Ontario, Canada.

SECOND PLACE

IN VERA VERITAS
©2018 by Ronna L. Edelstein

Vera ached all over, inside and out. After hours and days at her computer, her fingers, wrists, shoulders, and back cried out for a massage, but Vera knew that the relief from a massage would be short-lived and not worth her time or expense. Her head pounded as if a miniature drummer had taken up residence in her skull. The chronic aching caused by the prosthetic joint in her left jaw intensified her current pain. As her favorite poet, Langston Hughes, wrote, Vera felt like a broken- winged bird that could no longer fly.

What hurt the most, however, was her heart. It suffered from sadness—a deep-rooted sadness that refused to go away. Vera, who had just turned seventy, believed she had nothing to show for her life. Her son and daughter, both adults, grappled with constant challenges; neither had found a partner with whom to share their lives; the happiness of a family and security that Vera wanted them to have eluded them like the brass ring on the amusement park carousel. Not only did they both live far away, but their time-consuming jobs made it difficult for them to visit Vera, and Vera, who had a profound fear of flying, could not easily go to them. She lived alone in the condo her late beloved parents once owned and now contained their ghosts. Vera had tired of dinners, movies, and theatre outings with friends; adult education classes no longer excited her as they once had. After years of daily gym going, Vera had cancelled her membership and chosen to ride her stationary bike, turning the wheels round and round and never moving forward—an apt metaphor for her life.

Vera yearned for happiness just as a sojourner in the desert yearns for the distant spring of fresh water to be real, not another disappointing mirage. To find that happiness, Vera turned to make-believe. She had always used her imagination as an escape from reality: the dolls in the doll corner of her childhood basement had given her the companionship from which her more popular classmates deprived her; the Nancy Drew and other books lined up in the space on her headboard had offered her the adventures and success that did not happen in real life; with Ma's mah-jongg racks, she had built utopian villages where each person—embodied by one of the different colored tiles—had a place of prominence and an abundance of self-esteem.

Therefore, Vera decided to use her imagination to write a story. As always, she rooted her story in her life, this time focusing on college since she would soon celebrate her fiftieth anniversary of completing her undergraduate degree. Vera chose to re-visit her year with Anita, her freshman roommate, but in her story, she would rewrite reality by making her relationship with Anita the perfect one—and by making herself a congenial, amiable person. Not only would she and Anita enjoy a fabulous year together, but also, they would go on to be roommates throughout college and then become lifelong friends. Vera would leave the darkness of her life and of her memories by creating a bright story based on lies.

And so she wrote about how, three days before classes began, two eighteen-year-olds met in a corner dormitory room—one that received morning and afternoon light due to the placement of the windows. Nora, the fictional name she gave herself, and Allison, the pseudonym she assigned to her real roommate, had communicated throughout the summer, ever since the school notified them of their roommate assignment. As a result, the girls were prepared with matching comforters—a splash of soft blues and golden hues to complement the colors of the university—and agreed-upon pictures (Nora needed her big poster of Elvis above her desk, and Allison could not sleep without her photo of Paul McCartney over her bed). Even though Nora towered over the petite, dimpled Allison, the two managed to hug in a way that was comfortable without making Nora feel like a Brobdingnagian suffocating a Lilliputian. They stayed up late that first night, whispering to each other their dreams about college—Nora aimed for Phi Beta Kappa and Summa Cum Laude, while Allison hoped for an engagement ring and a summer wedding following graduation. Both girls were determined to make college the best years of their lives.

For the next few days, before classes, tests, and papers consumed them, Nora and Allison focused on enriching their social lives. Nora, having spent kindergarten through twelfth grade with the same people, had some friends who also attended the university and lived in her dorm. Similarly, Allison, despite traveling to the university from across the state, also knew half-a-dozen girls from her high school. The night before classes began, therefore, the two invited their forever girlfriends to the dorm room they shared. While sipping soft drinks, devouring pizza, and munching on the chocolate chip cookies Nora's grandma had baked and then Ma had packed in the tin can with the Andrew Wyeth's *Christina's World* decorated lid, they giggled about the guys they had seen on campus (so much cooler than the ones from high school), the communal bathroom (not as gross as they had envisioned), and the greasy dining hall food (beware the Freshman Fifteen). Sometimes Nora and Allison would look at each other and smile, secure in the belief that they were planting the seeds of a long and fruitful relationship. When the evening ended in a giggling rendition of *Kumbaya,* Nora did not let embarrassment caused by her off-key voice prevent her from joining in.

Everything that freshman year went smoothly. The same sorority tapped both Nora and Allison, turning the two into sisters as well as friends. They double-dated to the Spring Ball, admiring each other's colorful corsage and handsome escort. When Allison needed help studying for a psychology exam, Nora was there for her; when Nora required assistance in applying eyeliner, Allison was ready with her bag full of make-up. Everyone who knew the two girls marveled at their amazing friendship.

In this fictionalized version of reality, Vera disappeared within the character of Nora—the person Vera had always wanted to be. As Nora, she lived in social heaven and enjoyed the camaraderie of friends who did not label her the Jolly Green Giant, who did not tease her that her teeth, despite two years of wearing braces, were moving forward in an unattractive way, and who did not belittle her for knowing more Broadway tunes than the hit music so popular among teenagers. Nora was the ideal college roommate who made life for herself and Allison a grand adventure.

But this "grandness" is what Vera the writer struggled with, leading her and her throbbing body away from her computer to her blue recliner. Vera had wanted her story to be a Disney version of reality—a happily-ever-after that had no room for stifled silences, lethal looks, or angry actions—but she was failing. All that she had written the past week was a hodgepodge of clichés about best girlfriends forever, sorority parties, dates, and late-night conversations—things about which Vera knew nothing.

The longer she reclined on her chair, the more frustrated Vera became.

How could she realistically describe the Spring Ball that Nora and Allison went to together with their dates when she, Vera, had never gone to a formal dance—when she, Vera, could not dance and had never gone on a date? How could Vera possibly convey in a realistic way that Nora stayed up with Allison and their friends to the wee hours of the morning when Vera, whose only friends were books, had insisted that all lights in the room be off by 9 p.m. so she could get the sleep she needed in order to excel in school? How could she explain that Allison volunteered to remain roommates with Nora for the next three years, when all of the real Anita's friends decided to be "grown-ups" and live in apartments off-campus—and the real Vera had opted for a dorm that only had single rooms? For Allison and Nora to stand up at each other's wedding would require Nora/Vera to find a groom; that seemed as impossible as Allison/Anita, a student who struggled academically, managing to make the Dean's List.

How could Vera transform the real darkness of her freshman year into one of invented light? How could Vera present Nora as a popular, perky protagonist—a person that the real Vera would never ever be?

Vera distracted herself by scratching the sole of her right foot with the big toe of her left foot. Was an itchy foot a harbinger of money to come—or was it an itchy palm that promised a fortune? When the sole of her right foot began to bleed after a sharp edge of the nail on her big left toe tore the skin, Vera limped to the bathroom to put an antibiotic cream and a Band-Aid on the injury. She knew she also had to wrap a bandage around her efforts to fictionalize her story and herself. As her writing teachers always had told her, "Write about what you know"—and what Vera knew was pain, social exile, and loneliness, much of it self-induced. Hobbling back to her computer, Vera sat down and again began to write—this time a story about Vera and Anita, real names of real people, and how fate brought them together until Vera, incapable of being anything but a roommate from hell, tore them apart.

Vera and Anita were girls when they first met—eighteen-year-olds eager to embark upon their new life as college freshmen. When Vera had received the official letter of acceptance to her local university, she had been relieved that her poor standardized test scores, a stark contrast to her 4.0 GPA and column-long list of extracurricular activities, had not prohibited her from attending the school of her choice. Grandma was thrilled that Vera would live on campus but still be only a ten-minute drive from her apartment. Dad, who understood that Vera was a young and naïve teenager, was glad Vera would be nearby, but he worried that Ma would continue to control Vera's choices and life. Dad was right.

Vera's initial contact with Anita foreshadowed what would be a relationship of angst and alienation. Anita, who lived on the other side of the state, wrote a chirpy letter, one that Vera's classmates but not friends—the popular Linda, DeeDee, Judy, and Laura—could have written. She suggested that they buy bedspreads and accessories in cotton candy pink and soft gray. But Anita did not know that Ma had already bought Vera's comforter in a dark blue ("It will not show the dirt") with a dark gray trim ("To match the carpet") and that by the time Anita arrived on campus, Ma—and, by extension, Vera—would have turned the dorm room into one that fit Vera's needs and did not even recognize that Anita existed. Vera never responded to Anita's letter.

Two weeks before the term began, the university announced that the dorms would be open for freshmen to move in. Anita had indicated she would arrive later due to a family vacation at the beach, but that did not deter Ma from taking action. She stood on the sidewalk shortly after the sun had awakened and directed Vera and Dad on how to best load the car with linens, clothing, typewriter, radio, and other necessities for the room. By the time the sun had set, Vera had her clothes hanging in the larger of the two closets, her spread on the bed with the best view of the campus, and her typewriter sitting on the desk farther away from the door and the noise that would come from the hall. Her poster of Shakespeare hung above her desk.

Before getting into the car with Dad to go home, Ma turned to Vera and handed her a tin can, the one whose lid displayed Andrew Wyeth's *Christina's World*. "Grandma baked your favorite chocolate chip cookies, and I packed them," Ma told Vera. She then instructed Vera to "hide the tin can" because the cookies were just for her and not meant to be shared with her roommate. Vera obediently agreed to do as Ma said.

Several days later, when Anita finally arrived, Vera did not reach out to hug her. Anita's short, trim body, dimpled cheeks, and hair styled in a perfect flip made Vera cringe; the more she silently admired Anita's "cuteness," the more awkward and clumsy Vera felt. Vera sat silently on her bed and watched as Anita unpacked, casually threw her comforter on her bed, and filled her bookshelf with stuffed animals and a team picture of her with the other high school cheerleaders, not the dictionary, thesaurus, and other books that stood at attention on Vera's shelf. Then, with an "I'll be back" wave of her hand, Anita left the room.

By the time she returned, with half-a-dozen other girls in tow (it seemed that Anita's close high school friends had all chosen to attend the same university), Vera was in bed; her pink rollers pierced her skull, and dots of cold cream on her face made her look as if she had a strange case of chicken pox. Anita and her friends glanced at Vera, looked at the clock—it was 9 p.m., shrugged, and began chatting as if they had not seen each other in decades. They ignored Vera's pleas to "keep it down." Vera tried to escape their intrusive behavior by reading; she then opened the tin container next to her bed and nibbled on one of the chocolate chip cookies that Grandma had baked and Ma had packed for her. She scrutinized the lid, wondering what Wyeth's Christina pondered as she lay on the grass beyond her farmhouse. Did Christina resent her life of social aloneness, or had she found a sense of peace—one that evaded Vera—in who she was and how she lived? Christina did not offer Vera any insight into her thoughts.

Anita, smelling the delicious aroma of the cookies, asked Vera if she and her friends could have some. When Vera clutched the container to her chest and mumbled, "No," Anita looked at her with a mixture of incredulity and dismay. From that moment on, any hopes of a happy roommate situation crumbled.

Rather than respond to Vera's complaints about the messiness on her side of the room, insistence that she lower the volume of her radio to a whisper so Vera could study, and demand that the room go dark early in order for Vera to get a good night's rest, Anita spent most of the year wrapped in a sleeping bag on the floor of her friends' rooms. Although she never engaged in a direct conversation with Vera, Anita used angry monologues to let Vera know that living with her had led to a reoccurrence of her early high school acne and a sense of anxiety that had little to do with the academic challenges she faced. She made sure that Vera felt responsible for her low grades and her putting on weight due to tension. Anita blamed Vera for her failure to be accepted by any of the campus sororities. When Anita did not receive an invitation to the Spring Ball, something about which she had dreamed all year, she stole the tin of chocolate chip cookies—Ma delivered the fresh ones that Grandma baked every week when she came to get Vera's dirty laundry and return her clean and ironed clothes—and presumably devoured them with her loyal posse of friends. The tin with its *Christina's World* lid sat forlornly on Vera's bed; crumbs and a few bits of chocolate lay like pieces of sand and clumps of dirt on her bedspread. Weeks later, when Vera returned from taking her last final of the spring term, Anita had already packed and left. Vera never again saw Anita.

After completing her real story—with a whimper, not a bang—Vera returned to her blue recliner. She again felt an itch, but this itch was not coming from her right foot. Instead, it was an internal itch—a sudden need to find Anita and learn what had happened to her after that heinous freshman year. Had Vera, by scarring Anita's first year of college, ruined the rest of Anita's college career and life, or had Anita found a way to pursue and grasp happiness—to create a life rooted in a solid foundation of family and love that Vera had never enjoyed? A part of Vera, the part that believed that misery loves company, hoped that Anita's life had been a dismal one; another part, however, wanted Anita to have enjoyed the "Nora life" that had been Vera's dream.

Using technology, tidbits she had picked up from reading detective stories, and true grit—including making a long but futile call to the university's alumni office—Vera managed within four days to track down Anita. With shaking fingers, she dialed the number. Although the voice she heard sing "Hello" sounded older than that of a teenager, it still contained the perkiness that had defined Anita's speaking. After re-introducing herself to Anita, Vera explained that she wanted to apologize for freshman year and her odious behavior. Anita, however, seemed baffled. It was obvious to Vera that Anita's memories of freshman year were more nebulous than hers. Anita did not remember, or perhaps had successfully blocked, the invisible but thick wall Vera had erected between the two of them. She insisted that she did not recall that Vera had sat on her side of that wall, studying, reading, going to bed early, and getting up even earlier. She did not recall that Vera's selfishness and coldness had created a suffocating setting that squelched any hope of sisterhood.

Instead, Anita gushed about transferring to a different college her sophomore year—"I wanted to be closer to home"—and meeting and marrying a pre-law student; the two of them recently celebrated their 43rd . anniversary. Unlike Vera, who had struggled as a single mother to supply her children with all the necessities and some of the luxuries of life, Anita boasted about enjoying a financial security that did not demand that she contribute to the family's coffers by working as a social worker; she had used her time to volunteer at her two daughters' schools, at not-for-profit national organizations, and at many local charities. With a smile in her voice, Anita said that she and her husband traveled abroad at least once a year, and that they spent every August with their two daughters, sons-in-law, and three grandchildren at their summer home on the coast of New England.

Only when Vera stated that she sometimes dreamed of reuniting with Anita at the university, touring the expanded campus, and enjoying a snack of tea and chocolate chip cookies, did Anita stop speaking. The silence, which only lasted for seconds, seemed like eons to Vera. Apparently, her reference to the cookies had awakened something within Anita—a dark memory that had lain dormant for decades. Before Vera could speak, Anita abruptly ended the phone call by saying, "I remember things now—how you hoarded those cookies and made it impossible for me to be your friend. I remember how entering our dorm room felt like stepping into hell. Do not contact me again." Vera could almost hear Anita pound the "End" button on her cell phone.

Vera did not immediately hang up. When she did, she prayed that Anita would call her back and continue sharing stories of her golden life. Vera hungered for Anita's further assurance that she had not tainted Anita's life. Vera needed more proof that only she had suffered the consequences of her inability to be a friend to Anita, to all those unfortunate enough to cross paths with her—and to herself. The silence of her phone, however, deepened her ongoing debilitating headache, forcing Vera to place the phone on the table in defeat and curl up in her recliner.

Vera thought about the two stories—two different accounts of herself and one year in a life of seventy years—that she had begun to write. How she wished that her first version of her freshman year, the one starring Nora and Allison, had been the true story, not the mirage. Then, Vera could write about the lifelong friendship between Nora and Allison—how the two shared annual vacations with each other and their husbands, how their children built sand castles on the shore of Allison's summer house, how they met every year in Vegas or at a spa for a "girls' getaway" weekend, how they supported each other when their parents died.

But the real story of Vera and Anita made it impossible for Vera to find solace in the fictional one. Vera understood that her imagination offered her an escape from the daily grind of her life, but that the escape was only temporary. Inevitably, even if she convinced herself that Nora and Allison were real, Vera would have to return to the world of truth—where loneliness and hopelessness cast their constant shadows. Imagining a Nora/Allison life of happiness and togetherness was more heart-wrenching than accepting the truth of a "Vera life" of profound sadness and isolation. With a sudden spurt of energy, Vera got up, took the pages of the Nora/Allison story, and fed them to her shredder. The machine roared like an angry dragon when Vera turned it on; then, using its metal teeth, it destroyed the pages—the lies—into tiny strips of confetti.

Vera, overcome with exhaustion, collapsed one final time into her blue recliner, reached for the tin that always sat next to her chair—the image of Christina and the farmhouse on the lid had faded over the years and now suffered from scratches and rust— and grabbed a few chocolate chip cookies, the ones from the local grocery store that tasted stale even when they were fresh. The dry cookies, like the reality of her year with Anita, were hard to swallow, making Vera gag and choke. Even Christina, the woman depicted on the lid, looked more exhausted and feeble than she had when Vera had first admired the lid as a young child. Vera studied Christina, knowing that not even prayers would allow Christina's twisted legs and weakened arms to carry her home—or return the farmhouse, now a place of silence and unfulfilled dreams, into the happier house of Christina's past. So, too, did Vera stare into her past; she, a social cripple, realized that no amount of creative tampering with reality could change her history—or herself.

If only Vera could control real life people and situations like she could fictional characters and plots. If only fiction could comfort her rather than remind her of the brutal truths that lay behind it. If only Anita were sitting next to her, munching Grandma's cookies, enjoying Vera's company, and sharing pleasant memories. If only Vera could turn back the hands of the clock and start all over again—as Nora, the girl with possibilities.

Vera fell into a restless sleep, haunted by the "if onlys" of her life.

About the author:

As a part-time faculty member of the University of Pittsburgh's English Department, Ronna L. Edelstein works as a consultant at the school's Writing Center. She also teaches Freshman Programs, a course that introduces students to the University and the city. Her work, both fiction and nonfiction, has appeared in the following: "New Slang" A New Literary Voice by the Women and Girls of Pittsburgh" (online); *Quality Women's Fiction*; *Ghoti Online Literary Magazine*; *First Line Anthology*; *SLAB: Sound* and Literary Artbook; Pulse: Voices from the Heart of Medicine (online and print); AARP Bulletin (online and print); Healthy Roots (Forbes Health Foundation and Hospice); The Jet Fuel Review (Lewis University's online literary journal); Writer's Relief (online); Seasons of Caring; Tales of Our Lives: Fork in the Road (online e-book); Signature (Carnegie Mellon University Osher publication); Verse Envisioned: the Poetry and Art of Pittsburgh; the Washington Post; and the Pittsburgh Post-Gazette. "In Vera Veritas" is Ms. Edelstein's tenth Vera story to be accepted for publication by Scribes Valley Publishing.

THIRD PLACE

140 OVER 90
©2018 by Bill Mesce, Jr.

Lloyd didn't know how long Miriam had been standing in the living room archway but when he heard her long, slightly disgusted sigh, he had the impression it had been awhile.

"You're overdue," she said.

"Again with this?"

"I got a second email from the doctor's. And a text. And a phone call. You're overdue."

"I'm fine."

"Go for the physical."

"I'm fine."

"You are constantly whining this hurts, that hurts. You have enough pains to keep Bufferin in business for the next hundred years."

"Right now, the only pain I'm having is the one you're giving me in my ass."

"Go see your doctor. Get your physical. Maybe he can surgically separate you from the sofa."

"I'm fine."

She flapped her lips, wheeled around and headed toward somewhere in the back of the house. "Die early," she called back. "I don't care, the insurance is paid up, it's a payday for me."

Lloyd had wheezed his way through a few back and forth passes mowing the lawn before noticing his son sitting on the top porch step. Eddie's lips were moving but Lloyd couldn't hear him over the sound of the mower. He released the throttle bar and the motor died. "Did you say something?"

"You're sweating so much you look like you've been out in the rain."

"It's hot."

"It's not *that* hot."

"Did you want something?"

"Well, it's just it's hot—"

"Didn't I just say that?"

"—and you look like you're suffering... I'm worried, you know, like, you keel over or something, it'd be nice someone is here."

"Your mother send you out here?"

"Dad, I care."

"How much do you want?"

"No, I'm serious. Especially since you had those pull-ups in your keister."

"You mean polyps?"

"Whatever. Those things can, you know, kill you."

"Everybody gets polyps. It's no big deal."

"I worry, Dad. Can't I worry?"

"You're worried so much, *you* mow the lawn."

"That's not what I'm talking about."

"I know."

"Look, if it'll make you feel better, you go for the physical and I'll, you know, like, I'll drive you."

"How does that make me feel better? You've had your permit three days; you'll get us killed taking me for my physical. Wait a minute; is that what this is about? You get an excuse to take the Caddy out?"

"You know something, Dad? You got a bad attitude. You always think—"

"Ok, so let's say I say yes, I make the appointment, you get to drive me—"

"Great!"

"Hey, wait a second, I didn't say—"

Eddie was already halfway through the front door into the house. "I'm gonna call Julie."

"Who the hell is—"

"You don't mind she takes the ride with us, right?"

Julie came bouncing down the walk of her house in pink sneakers, stuck her metaled mouth in the passenger window and squeaked, "So you're Lloyd!"

"I'm Lloyd."

"Well, hello, Lloyd!" She had a ring in her nose, her hair cut into zebra stripes, and a ragged T-shirt with what looked like hand-painted scrawl reading, *Splatter Pattern Tour '15*. According to the tour stops listed on the T-shirt, the Splatter Pattern Tour of 2015 evidently consisted of a single date at a local pizzeria/saloon. She bounced into the back seat, blew a kiss to Eddie and squeaked, "Let's see whatcha got Eee-dee." That's what she called Eddie: Eee-dee. Lloyd didn't know why.

Every time Eee-dee ran a stop sign, halted too far into an intersection, or drifted over the lane lines, Julie seemed to think it was pee-in-your-pants funny. She giggled a squeaky giggle, sometimes threw in a squeaky scream as she bounced around the back seat. "Jesus, Eee-dee, do you even know, like, what you're doing?"

Eddie would bobble his head, let his tongue loll out of his mouth, and jiggle the steering wheel spastically. "Duh, duh, maybe I don't, duh."

"Eddie, don't horse around," Lloyd said, his right hand in a death grip on the arm rest.

"Whaddaya think, Jules," Eddie said, doing his moron face in the rearview. "Think they should give me my license? Duh duh."

"Eddie! Watch the road!"

39

The car started to drift over the center line, a horn screamed, a driver screamed, and Eddie screamed, "Asshole!" as he yanked the car back on course. "What's his fucking problem?"

"Mouth, Eddie."

"Oh, Jeez!" Julie said. She was excited about something and her squeaks jumped an octave making Lloyd wince. "Just imagine, like, you know, we get in an accident—"

I can easily imagine that, Lloyd thought.

"—and, like, we're all unconscious, you know? And our IDs are all messed up with, like, all the blood, right? They're gonna think I'm with you! Like, I'm one of the family! Hey, Lloyd, want a daughter?"

"No."

"Oh, wow!" She was really enthused now, on a roll, in the sound range of a dentist's drill. "What if, like, oh *wow,* we all *died* together! And they bury me with you guys 'cause they think I'm, like, you know, your daughter and stuff! And then we're, like, you know, in another existence, like a Heaven only it's not Heaven, and 'cause I got, like, buried with you guys, over there in the other universe I *am* your daughter!"

She's right, thought Lloyd, that's not Heaven.

"Jules wants to be a writer," Eddie said as if that explained anything. "Well, not, like, books or stuff like that." Which did explain things for Lloyd. "You know, it's, what? Anime, right? Isn't that what you want to do, Jules? Write anime?"

"Miyazaki is, like, a *god!*"

Lloyd wasn't listening at that point. "Stop sign, Eddie, stop sign, stop sign *stop sign!*"

"Your blood pressure's up," Lloyd's doctor said, pumping the bulb for the BP cuff for a second reading.

"I can't imagine why," Lloyd said.

Lloyd's doctor frowned at the second result and unwrapped the cuff. "I don't like that. You know what you can do to help bring that down?"

"Move to Tahiti?"

"I'm not laughing, Lloyd," and the doctor gave Lloyd's belly a couple of pokes. "Thirty pounds. I'd settle for twenty, but thirty would be better."

Lloyd looked down at his doctor's belly. The shirt button over the doctor's navel was straining so tight, if it popped Lloyd knew it would perforate him completely, embedding itself in the wall behind him. According to the anatomical chart on the wall, Lloyd saw the trajectory would take the button through Lloyd's small intestine and rupture his appendix before it blasted out his back.

"I'm going to leave the name of a nutritionist at the front desk for you. Make sure you pick it up when you leave. Ok, now, I'm going to make you the best offer you've had all day: drop your pants and bend over."

Lloyd's doctor made the same joke every physical. It was never funny and sure as hell didn't make what was to follow any more pleasant.

Lloyd bent over the examining table, winced at the snap of rubber gloves, felt his whole body tighten at the sound of the rotating cap on a jar of Vaseline.

"Ready?"

"No."

"Hmph. Relax."

"I'm trying. What're you doing, digging for the Higgs Boson?"

"I'm impressed. What do you know about the Higgs Boson?"

"I know it's not up there."

"Those yours?" The nurse at the front desk nodded to Eddie and Julie pointing at the other patients in the waiting room and giggling.

"Depends," Lloyd said. "What'd they do?"

"Just remember to take them with you when you leave. Here's that nutritionist information and a referral."

Lloyd handed over his parking receipt. "Could you validate this for me?"

The nurse blinked. "Excuse me?"

"Could you validate my parking?"

"Somebody in the lot charged you for parking?"

"Were they not supposed to do that?"

The nurse turned to another nurse fiddling with files nearby. "Hey, Irma, I think ol' Bennie's at it again."

The second nurse asked Lloyd what the guy in the parking lot looked like.

"Old guy, only had about half his teeth, sitting on a little stool next to a sign that said, 'Parking five dollars.'"

The nurses nodded. "That's Bennie."

"You're telling me he's not gonna be out there when I go out there."

"Doubtful," the one nurse said.

"Which means I'm not getting my five dollars back."

"Even more doubtful."

On the way out of the doctor's office, Lloyd conscientiously stuffed the nutritionist information and the referral note and his useless parking ticket in a recycling bin, then took the car keys from Eddie saying the deal was for Eddie to drive him *to* the doctor. Lloyd would drive them home.

Eddie and Julie sat together in the back seat. Eddie went into a cartoony act of trying to look down the low collar of Julie's T-shirt. "Duh, duh, what the heck are those things?" Julie, squeaking like an unoiled bicycle, would bat at his hands, laughing.

"Really, Eddie?" Lloyd said. "You have to do that in front of me?"

"I'm just kidding, for God's sake, Dad. She knows I'm kidding, right, Jules?"

"Don't take it so serious, Lloyd," Jules said.

Jesus, the boy's a cunning little shit, Lloyd thought, with an equal mix of disgust and admiration. He pulls the semi-retarded just-fooling-around thing, but that still gets him a look at this girl's boobs.

"I'm gonna stop at the bakery," Lloyd said. "Get bread for dinner."

"Yeah, sure," Eddie said. *"Bread."* Then he whispered something to Julie and both of them started squeaking together.

Lloyd pulled up at the curb in front of the bakery and climbed out of the car.

"You didn't ask if we, like, wanted something?" Eddie asked.

"You can have anything you can pay for."

"Uh—"

"Bye."

As Lloyd stepped up to the counter, he could see through a doorway into the kitchen where a young girl was baking cookies, the big hand-sized ones. She was pulling a just-done tray out of the oven, and the aroma of those fresh-baked lovelies—chocolate chip it smelled like—filled the bakery. Lloyd could feel his mouth juicing up.

The counter woman stepped up to him and Lloyd ordered a loaf of French bread.

"Anything else?"

The fresh-baked-cookie smell was still heavy in the bakery, stewing up nicely with the smell of fresh bread and fresh cakes and fresh pastries.

"Um," Lloyd said. He was looking down at a tray of éclairs lined up like heart-killing torpedoes. They looked damn fine and Lloyd thought the day he'd had so far had earned him a treat.

The woman in the kitchen started buttering up the cookie tray for a second load. Watching the woman dip into a tub of butter reminded him of his doctor greasing up his rubber gloves.

Lloyd made a little grunting noise.

"I'm sorry," the counter woman said, leaning in. "Did you say something?"

Lloyd shook his head. "I'm good." He turned for the door and saw Eddie and Julie horsing around in the car, something that involved Eddie jumping back and forth over the front seat and Jules playfully yelling "Rape!" out the window. Lloyd had a brief vision of sneaking out the bakery's back door and walking home.

He reached for the loaf of French bread, then remembered Eddie liked chocolate chip cookies.

"Let me have one of those chocolate chip numbers, the big one there." Then he thought of Julie though it pained him to think of Julie and he said, "Better make it two."

He remembered Miriam liked the ones with almonds and vanilla chunks and he ordered one of those, too.

About the author:

Bill Mesce, Jr., a native New Jerseyan, is a sometime author, occasional screenwriter, even more occasional playwright. He is currently on the Creative Writing faculty at the University of Maine at Farmington. Prior, he was an adjunct at a number of New Jersey colleges and universities. Before teaching, he spent 27 years in Corporate Communications at pay-TV giant Home Box Office.

WUNNER IF ELVIS GOT THE GUN INSTEAD?
©2018 by Mike Tuohy

Mr. Bobo winced when the lady told the boy they lacked the money for the bicycle. He was ready when they approached the counter. "Heard you're quite the singer, Elvis. What you need is a guitar." He handed the boy a shiny six string.

The boy admired the wood grain on the body and twisted a couple of the tuning pegs. He picked a few sour notes and grinned up at his mother as he strummed.

She touched her fingertips to her temple. The headache she woke up with worsened. "Maybe we can get Preacher Smith to give you some lessons."

Mr. Bobo forced a smile. "He's a natural talent, Gladys."

The strumming stopped. The birthday boy was transfixed by a .22 caliber rifle mounted on the wall. "Mama, I wouldn't need no lessons to shoot a gun. I could practice on them rabbits been eatin' your garden."

"No, honey. It's dangerous." Gladys looked to Mr. Bobo for support, but he was called away to cut a key.

Elvis gently placed the guitar on the counter. "When Daddy's away, I could protect the house."

"Maybe when you're twelve. That's a more proper age."

"But, Mama! The Anderson's house got broke into last week." He looked up with those big, wet eyes.

Gladys pondered for a moment. The headache would not be going away as long as this continued. "You promise me that you won't shoot anything other than varmints or bottles?"

The boy's lip trembled. "I will swear to God on the Holy Bible, Mama."

Mr. Bobo returned. "Now, you want some picks to go with that guitar?"

Mrs. Presley put her hand on Elvis' shoulder. "My little man here prefers the rifle for his birthday."

Mr. Bobo pursed his lips, slid the guitar aside and laid the gun in its place. "Well, I'm sure you have raised him to be a responsible young man."

Elvis pressed up against the counter and ran a finger along the metal barrel and wooden stock. "Oh, yes sir, Mr. Bobo. I won't shoot nothin' that don't need shootin'."

"I suppose you'll want ammunition with that?"

Elvis' eyes widened. "That extra?"

"You better know it. Long rifle loads or shorts?"

Gladys jumped in. "Shorts quieter?"

"Yes, ma'am."

"Make it shorts."

"But, Mama!"

Mr. Bobo winked at Gladys and looked at Elvis. "They're cheaper, son. More bang for your buck."

Elvis shrugged, picked up the rifle and grinned. "Them rabbits ain't got a chance."

A week later, hardly a squirrel, bunny or chipmunk remained within a one-hundred-yard radius of the Presley's Tupelo home. Frustrated after an hour with nothing to shoot at but a dead possum, the boy headed to nearby Mud Creek. The hunting was bound to be better or at least more tolerable in the shade of the Main Street bridge. Killing some water moccasins would surely make the world a better place.

Elvis had a muskrat in his sights when he and it were startled by a sharp guitar chord and a moan followed by a hacking cough. A white-haired black man with a cigar box guitar sat on an overturned bucket not twenty feet to his left.

Elvis turned to the stranger. "Excuse me, sir. I didn't see you there."

The man smiled, more gums than teeth. "Not your fault, Mr. Elvis. I kind of blend into the shade."

Elvis knew this sometime handyman who lived nearby. "Why, Mr. Clifford! Fancy meeting you here."

"Coolest spot in town, at least in the daytime."

Elvis laughed. "Well, I'm down here to rid this town of vermin."

Clifford twisted the screws on his instrument with a pocket knife. "Ain't nothin' down here but God's creatures doin' what they was created for."

"What do you mean?"

Clifford shrugged. "Birds got to fly. Bees got to sting."

Elvis sat down on the edge of an old tractor tire and pressed his face against the rifle barrel. "What about snakes? You okay they bite you?"

Clifford smiled. "Snakes is different. They of the devil. Shoot all Mr. No Shoulders you want." He strummed his makeshift guitar, turned two screws and did it again.

Elvis dipped his head. "Now, that does sound a little better. How does that work?"

Clifford extended one hand. "Gimme that rifle, son."

Elvis obeyed. Clifford set the rifle butt on one knee and the cigar box body of the guitar on the other.

"Now, you see here, we got two things, each a marriage of wood and metal. Steel strings. Steel barrel. Wood sound box. Wood stock. Got it?"

Elvis nodded.

"Now, pay attention." The old man took aim at a Cooter-encrusted log. With a *crack* from the rifle, a one-foot section at the tip of the log dropped into the water. The rest of the turtles immediately followed. With three more shots, he shortened the log another foot. "Hear that? Bang. Bang. Bang"

"That's some mighty fine shootin'."

Clifford handed the gun back, put a sawed-off bottle neck on a finger and picked up his instrument. "Now, listen to this." Picking the strings as he slid the glass up and down the neck of the guitar, he teased out a tune with a sound Elvis had never heard before.

Elvis grinned. "That's good stuff, Mr. Clifford. What's that called?"

"Robert Johnson thing. *Riverside Blues* or some such." He handed the gun back to the boy. "So, which you think you'd rather have now?"

Elvis pulled the rifle close to his chest. "Can't say I could help feed my family with a guitar."

Clifford leaned back. "Ain't you a little young to be thinking about havin' a family?"

Elvis blushed. "I meant my momma and daddy, but I suppose I'll have me one of my own someday."

"Nothin' wrong with thinking ahead. So, you like girls, Elvis?"

The boy grinned. "They're all right, I suppose."

"Now, tell me which sounds better." Clifford grabbed the rifle and stood up. Cradling the gun in the crook of his arm, he held a fist sideways, tilted his head, letting his tongue loll out one side of his mouth as he spoke in a hillbilly voice. "Hey, baby! I done brung you a squirrel."

Elvis leaned his elbows on his knees and laughed hard. When he sat back up, Clifford stood before him, holding the guitar by the neck.

"Or this." He turned one leg out at an odd angle and his upper lip curled into a sneer. His voice went deep. "Hey, baby. I done wrote you a song."

For the next few minutes, Elvis sat in awe as he was treated to a slide rendition of *Roll and Tumble Blues*. He was as amazed by the voice that came out of the old man's body and even more by what came out of the makeshift instrument.

At the end of the song, Clifford smiled, pulled a dirty red kerchief from his overalls and wiped the sweat from his forehead. "Of course, if I had more than four strings, I could do it a little more justice."

"That was real good, Mr. Clifford. Real good." Dazed, Elvis picked up his rifle and headed home.

At the sound of the door chimes, Mr. Bobo looked up from the cash register. "Elvis! Good to see you, son! Back for some more bullets?"

Elvis looked down as he handed up the rifle-sized box and mumbled. "No, sir. I was hoping I could trade this in."

Mr. Bobo accepted the box and laid it on the counter. "Your birthday rifle? I hope it was not defective."

"Oh, no sir! It worked just fine. I rid the town of many critters we could do without. It's just that somebody pointed out a problem with guns."

Mr. Bobo looked from side to side and tilted his head at the riddle. "What would that be, son?"

"Well, sir, seems it don't play but one note. *Bang*."

Mr. Bobo nodded. "Whoever told you that is a wise man. I don't suppose you'll be wanting that guitar after all?"

Elvis looked up hopefully. "If you don't mind, Mr. Bobo. I know the rifle's used now, but I'll pay or work off the difference. I cleaned and oiled her real good."

Mr. Bobo held up and examined the gun with care. "You sure did, Elvis." He slid the rifle to one side and put the guitar in its place. "We'll call it even. Now, go make your mama proud."

About the author:

A bottle-fed Baby Boomer, Mike moved from New Jersey to Georgia in 1965, and has been soaking up Southern culture ever since. After decades working the environmental consulting racket as a geologist, Mike uses his semi-retirement to capture a lifetime of observations and evolving philosophy in the guise of fictional short stories, flash fiction, novellas and a novel. In addition to 23 published short works, he has twice been a finalist in The New Yorker Cartoon Caption Contest, getting a total of nine words in that prestigious publication. Mike's website, bunker93a.com, serves as his manifesto and showcase for his work.

JOYS
©2018 by Lucy Marcus

Today Estelle would do it, and not for anyone but herself: she would organize the papers. She would go through each pile and make some order out of their madness. Sort them in such a way as to simplify the finding of things. Chronology never mattered. She'd do it by theme. She brainstormed the categories as she stretched in bed, still in her nightgown, her hands clasped over her chest. She thought of three piles to start with: "Life Extension Strategies" for health advice; "Different Ways of Living," for style and cultures around the world; and her favorite, "Controversial Conflicts," a category which spoke for itself. But where to put the obituaries? She wiggled her toes at the end of the bed, little animals beneath her blankets. One more pile for obituaries and other news of tragedies, and dated articles that outlived their subjects. Call it "Death." Yes, four piles to start, that would be feasible.

She threw off her blankets, stood up, and began to make the bed. The sheets, once white, were yellowed and full of tiny holes. As she folded the bottom sheet under the mattress, she noticed a crease. She reached under to find a crumbled article about flu shots. She had snipped it from the Health section the previous night. Recent research showed that a good mood could boost the flu shot's effectiveness. She felt a pressing anxiety to inform her daughters. They were always in bad moods. She checked the time: 7:15AM, too early to call Alma or Susan, but Julia, her youngest, would be awake. She pressed out the article's wrinkles on her belly and placed it on her night table by the phone. She dialed Julia's number. "Juju," she said, after the ringing paused. "Have you seen the article about flu shots in Wednesday's paper?"

"No, Ma. Is it urgent?"

"They found that you need to be in a good mood for the shot to work. You have to start meditating, I'll give you my mantra if you need one." Estelle grabbed a pen and began to doodle a face on the border of the article. "And you won't believe what happened. The landlord threatened me! I tried calling you yesterday evening but you didn't answer. I was so worried."

"Oh, really?"

Estelle could hear porcelain clattering and the faraway sound of her granddaughter calling for Julia's attention. "Are you listening to me? I woke up so depressed. He wants to confiscate the newspapers."

"You have to do something about that," Julia said over the sound of running water, "It's out of control."

"You sound distracted," Estelle said. "Call me later, please. And don't get a flu shot if you're in a bad mood!"

"Love you," her daughter said before hanging up.

Her daughters had begged her to organize the newspapers for years. Only yesterday, when her landlord invaded her apartment to tend a leaky radiator, did she consider their request. The landlord scolded and threatened her. If she didn't remove the papers, which he declared a fire hazard, he would come do it himself. They were so rude to her, the building's management. They had no respect. She had lived in the building longer than they'd been alive, and still they tortured her with angry tones, demanding something with every interaction. First, they wanted to take down her paintings from the hallway and now the belongings in her own home. No respect and no privacy. If she wasn't a rent-controlled tenant, they would grovel to her, they would kiss her cheeks each time she walked through the double glass doors of the refurbished lobby. But no, to them she was a liability, a profit thief, a bleeding wallet.

She retrieved the morning's paper, which was waiting outside of her door, folded and eager to be read. She brought it in, ran her hands over the fresh print, and placed it on the dining room table, where she cleared a little rectangle of space by piling up the other papers. She would sort those later. She made her coffee and smeared a piece of wheat bread with jam. As she ate her breakfast, she began to read.

A Palestinian man was killed by Israeli forces at a peaceful protest, leaving behind twelve-year-old twin daughters. The incident ignited protests all over the West Bank. The article showed an image of a young boy carrying a poster with the portrait of the killed man. The man was handsome, with a sharp jaw and soft eyes and loose brown curls. She put down her bread and reread the article. Her granddaughter, Alma's eldest, had just spent the summer in Israel. Estelle's own father fought for the creation of Israel over fifty years ago. She admired him as a girl but had since renounced Zionism. Her daughters, however, did not. Blinded by the stories their father, Bernard, told them, Estelle supposed. Yes, her ex-husband's parents lived through the Holocaust but history moved and turned and even Bernard was dead. It was the paper that opened Estelle's eyes. She was sure that if her daughters read the articles, if they saw the violence, they would agree with her. They didn't like discussing the subject but she'd have to break through their denial.

It was 8:30AM now, late enough to call Alma. Estelle flipped through her contact book and found Alma's new cell phone number. It was such a wonderful invention, the cell phone—to reach Alma anywhere! At this moment, she would be walking from the subway into work. The phone rang twice, then jolted to voicemail. Her own daughter's voice, cold and professional. That was the curse of the cell phone: you could screen the call. Was Alma ignoring her? She left a message anyway: "Hi dear, have you read this morning's paper? Read the article about Israel and Palestine. There are protests. It's not safe to go there, make sure you tell the girls. There was an innocent man, murdered! And leaving two daughters fatherless, daughters the same age as Lily. Can you imagine? I don't know how you can justify what that government is doing. He was peaceful, killed in the crossfire, and now they call him a terrorist. It's in the paper, please read it and get back to me as soon as you can. Love you, dear." She hung up, feeling a tinge of accomplishment.

A moment later, she dialed Alma's cell phone again, remembering the original news of the flu shot. She got the voicemail after one ring. She left another message: "It's your mother. Call me back. I'm worried about you. I forgot to tell you something very important about the flu shot from yesterday's paper. Don't get a shot until you speak with me! It's urgent. Love you, my dear."

Estelle put down the phone and felt consumed by anxiety. It had been several days since she spoke with Alma. She sometimes doubted her daughters even listened to the messages. Or, if they did listen, they were probably laughing at her, mocking her with their caring husbands and rosy-cheeked daughters by their sides while she was all alone. Abandoned by Bernard the bastard. How could they let her be alone, after everything she'd given them? Those four hot, sweaty years in San Juan, heartbroken, delirious, broke! He left her for a busty, big-hipped woman, and not even a Jew! A young, childless woman. The humiliation! Left her with three young girls, far from family, hardly speaking a word of Spanish. And how did she even end up there? It was his doing, but she'd since forgotten why. Something with the business and the books and bankruptcy. It would come to her. She just had to give it time and it would come. She wished she had an article about it in the papers. But of course, if there was one, she probably wouldn't be able to find it. That was the issue with the papers. Gone when you wanted it. Buried somewhere unfound.

She left a message for Susan, her eldest daughter, who she hadn't spoken with in weeks. Yes, her daughters neglected her, and when they did call she often had a vague suspicion that they wanted something from her, almost always to watch their children. She loved the grandchildren, they were precious and delightful and full of love, but she wanted to be wanted by grown people, too. She couldn't understand why they'd be angry with her. They were, of course, the most important thing in her life, and their welfare the most crucial. She hoped now that they had children of their own they could understand her feelings (and, she had to admit to herself, experience some rejection too). Maybe then they'd be less cruel to her. Their insensitivity made her furious, and when she'd express her fury, they'd stop answering her calls. Without speaking to them, she'd grow depressed and lonely. After a few days, she'd apologize to them in chaptered voice massages, her tone sweet and gentle. By the time they called her back, she'd forget why she was mad at them in the first place.

Memory, that was another reason why she loved the papers. They remembered what she forgot. A whole world chronicled, a whole day's worth of global events documented forever. She wondered if she'd be documented in the paper one day. One day, yes, she would. In fact, she already had been. She still had the article somewhere, from 1964. A reporter interviewed her as she stood in her Puerto Rico studio with the girls. All three of them with her, paintbrushes in hand, painting smocks over their little bodies. She remembered picking it up from her porch, and how she forgot about the heat as she read the article in the sun, how in that moment, briefly, she forgot all about Bernard the bastard. But then, afterwards, thoughts of him returned—had he seen it, what did he think, did her waist look thin? Did her nose look big? Was he jealous? She hoped he was jealous. She sent a copy of the article with each of the girls as they went to visit their father for the weekend, "Just to catch him up on what you've been up to, not that he'll care or anything, too busy with his young new girlfriend, but show it to him anyway, why not?"

She cleared her dish and cup, scrubbing violently as she thought about goddamned Bernard. Twelve years buried in a cloudy graveyard on the edge of the Bronx, and still she thought about him at least every day. The bastard. Her daughters forbid her from speaking about their father, a rule she struggled to follow. She tried, but without speaking, the thoughts of him bubbled up in her head until there was nothing else she could think of. She'd return to the paper, read about an injustice somewhere near or far, it didn't matter. Soon enough she'd feel a violent wrath at the oppressors and the ensuing need to communicate the injustice with those around her. That's when she'd pick up the phone and call her daughters. "You have to read this," she'd say, most likely into the answering machine. "Page eight, Section B." And just in case they didn't bother to read it, she'd summarize the main points.

She grabbed her scissors and cut out the article about the boy. She snipped words from the headline: "MURDER," "MOURNING," "UPRISING." She changed into her painting clothes, a faded and ripped maternity smock splattered with acrylic blues, whites, and yellows. She took her snippets, put on her slippers, and went into the studio. She was pleasantly surprised to find a new blank canvas she must have stretched the day before. It was a sign, time for a new painting. She turned on her paint-splattered boom box to the classical radio station. A somber piano duet filled her stomach with a buzzing, echoing energy that spread up to her shoulders, and neck and arms, then down into her shaking hands. She squeezed black paint into a leftover Chinese takeout container, a shallow one that once held sweet, sticky brown sauce. She grabbed a brush and began.

Oil spills. Lavas of longing left untouched, unmet, hardened into fossilized scars. She pasted the newspaper cutouts onto the canvas and stabbed a paint sample of red on the bottom left with a tack. Paste, brush, pierce. Paste, brush, pierce. Her hands moved in a rhythm of their own to the staccato, the marching of men, war. Tacks littered the floor at her feet as they escaped her shaking fingers. Her hands grew sticky with glue and black with paint.

Paste, brush, pierce. She thought of the man, his funeral, the crying mothers, wailing. She thought of Bernard, dead, dead, dead. Bernard the bastard, half of her daughters' genes. Her daughters, the greatest joys of her life, and he couldn't even leave them be. He had to ruin, ruin, ruin. Paste, brush, pierce. In their anger, Estelle knew it was Bernard and his horrendous, psychopathic, emotionless blood pumping quicker and stronger and redder than her own. Paste, brush, pierce. Oh, how she hated him. She squeezed a line of thick, greasy orange directly onto her black brush so that black ash tarnished the color's edges. She swiped it, breathless and exhilarated, in a diagonal over the whole canvas, over the words and cutouts and black, the orange a brilliant flame.

She put down the brush and wiped her forehead, wet with sweat. She looked down at her hand and saw the black residue. She laughed at herself. Each session in the studio, she always managed to get paint on her face. She left the studio with the boom box still playing and walked to the bathroom. She wet a tissue and wiped her face with it, its thin paper disintegrating onto her skin. Before she could clean it off, the phone rang. She nearly fell over a heap of papers as she ran to it.

"Yes, hello, this is Estelle, who is this?" she said, winded.

"It's me," said Julia.

"Oh, thank God you're all right."

"Why wouldn't I be?" Her voice curved into sharp edges, impatient.

"Did you read the article about the flu? And have you read today's paper? An innocent man murdered." Estelle grabbed her pen and pad next to the phone and began to doodle spirals, going over the lines again and again. "He was innocent, and the IDF shot him, he was only playing around. And did I tell you I was just in the studio? A burst of energy got me painting! A new piece, not sure what I'll call it, maybe something with Holocaust, I'm not sure yet, I can't wait for you to see it—"

"I forgot to remind you that Chesed is today. Did you remember?" Julia said. "A lady is coming to pick you up at three."

Estelle panicked: she *had* forgotten. Chesed was the day care center for the Jewish elderly. She went every week and participated, begrudgingly, in the infantile craft activities planned by young volunteers.

"I can't today, Juju," Estelle said. "I have too much to do. I still have to organize my papers."

"Ma, please," Julia said. "The lady is probably on her way. It's too late to cancel, please."

Estelle's spirals were as thick as fat snakes, the ink bleeding into the pages beneath.

"And I'm covered in paint! I'll never be ready in time."

Julia sighed. "Ma, I have to go. Please, the lady will help you get ready." Her daughter hung up without waiting for a reply.

Estelle ran back to the bathroom, stepping over the spilled papers in her path. She looked at herself in the mirror: little pieces of tissue stuck to her gray forehead, sweat bubbled on her upper lip, her nose in need of powdering. A mess! She wanted to look nice for Chesed. There was a man there, a potential gentleman caller. He asked her out on a date weeks ago, his aide standing next to him, her aide standing next to her, both of them smiling at each other like amused parents of mischievous children. The humiliation! She had no choice but to say yes. The trouble was, she couldn't remember who this man was. White hair, wisps of it, glasses, but the rest was a blur. She wouldn't dare lose her dignity by asking her aide, and besides, it was a new lady almost every week. She already forgot who the aide was that day. And so she was forced to greet every gentleman with a ladylike familiarity, the tone of a woman just asked out on a date. It had been six weeks and no man had since followed up with an additional invitation. Perhaps the man forgot about her, too. Perhaps he was embarrassed by his own forgetfulness. Or perhaps he had died. She had since tried looking for him in the obituaries but then she'd remember that she didn't know his name.

She ran back to the phone and called up her daughter, only to get the answering machine. "Please, Julia. Tell the lady not to come today. I'm under the weather. I can't go. There's no way!" She could hear the anger in her voice. She tried to soften it. "Please, Juju, call me back. I love you."

She looked at the time, it was after 1:00PM. She pressed a hand to her stomach, recognizing its rumbling, which had been resounding, a forgotten alarm, for nearly an hour. She went to the kitchen and prepared her midday smoothie, tossing walnuts and frozen fruits and yogurt into the blender. The loud roar of it silenced her panic. It was important to appreciate what she had, she reminded herself. Those poor children left fatherless, that innocent, handsome man murdered, forgotten, no time to make his mark. No time to create, to show the world the magic of his mind. No time to fall in and out of love and grow old. Alone, he died. Alone, dead, alone. She poured the smoothie into a tall glass and carried it with her to the bedroom. She took intermittent sips of the thick liquid as she began to ready herself for Chesed.

Her aide today was a thin Polish woman with wiry brown hair. She stood as Estelle sat in the empty seat on the bus reserved for the elderly. It was a new woman, and she had already forgotten her name. Something with an M and an A. She was on her cell phone, typing into its tiny keyboard, hanging onto the bar above Estelle's seat so that her long floral skirt brushed over Estelle's knees.

In the chaos of leaving the apartment, she forgot to bring a paper to read on the bus. She ruffled through her pocketbook and pulled out a compact mirror and lipstick. When she looked up from the mirror, her lips a shade deeper, she saw a young boy looking at her across the aisle. His feet swung off the floor as he kicked them into the air. Next to him, his grandmother was asleep, her chin falling forward onto her enormous bosom.

Estelle smiled at the boy. She waved at him, a tissue in her hand, and he waved back, shy. "Hello," she said. Before he could reply, the bus jolted forward, jerking the aide, still on her cell phone, so that she stood between Estelle and the boy. "Excuse me," Estelle said, pulling at the woman's skirt. "Can you please move?"

The lady looked up from her phone, startled. "Get up!" she said. "Get up! Our stop!"

By the time they arrived to Chesed she was covered in sweat. Her shoulders ached. She wanted to go home. Chesed's elderly activities took place on the first floor of an office building. The linoleum floors and windowless walls gave off the sterile appearance of a hospital waiting room. She sat at an empty table and began to use the stickers of snowmen on one of the blank pieces of paper they scattered in front of each seat. Her aide sat across from her, back on her cell phone. Estelle took one of the markers and began to doodle spirals around the snowman. It was still autumn, the wrong season for snowmen, but who cared? She looked around at the old ladies of the other tables, chatting without looking at each other, probably unaware of the season.

A man tapped her shoulder. "May I?" he said, pointing to the folded chair next to hers. She nodded. She waited a moment, watching his hands reach for some stickers, before turning to look at his face. He was younger than she was, probably by a decade. White stubble coated his neck and chin, a knit brown hat sat snugly on his head. He felt her gaze and turned to her, his eyes big and blue.

"Hello," he smiled. She smiled, nervous.

"Did you see the article in *The Times* today about the murdered Palestinian man?" She spoke quickly, turning back to her art project.

"I don't read the paper," he said, tapping the table, a snowman stuck to his pointer finger. "Print's too small."

"He left behind two twin daughters, only twelve years old," she continued. "It's a tragedy. The Israeli forces shot him. Even though he had no weapons."

"Everyone's shooting everyone over there," he said, placing the sticker in the center of his blank page. "My brother's whole family lives in Tel Aviv. I pray for them every day."

"They should move here," Estelle said. "It's very dangerous there."

"It's beautiful," the man said. "Have you been?"

"Never. And I never will."

"No family over there?"

"None that I know of, thank God," her black doodles expanded, filling the white space of the page.

"What you don't know can't hurt you," he said.

She looked up at him. "No, that's not true," she shook her head. "Not true at all."

"Tell me," he said, his tone growing sharper. "Why do you concern yourself in all that trouble when you have no people there?" The man, she could tell, was angry. It had taken longer than the others, but he was not immune.

"Do you only care for your own? Where are they now?" She put down her pen.

"That's none of your business," he said.

"And why are you even speaking to me?" she felt the ticklish feeling of being right. "You don't know me!"

"Well I thought you were a nice-seeming Jewish lady. But you're apparently of the self-loathing variety!" With that, he stood, clutching his art project with both hands, and moved to the table behind hers, where the other ladies sat. They looked up at him with hungry eyes and made room, adjusting their chairs in a cacophony of scraping. When he sat, they gushed over his art piece, passing it around and pecking at it like flirtatious chickens.

She turned back in front of her to find the Polish aide looking up from her cell phone.

"That man was trying to be nice," the aide said.

"I want to go home," Estelle said. "Take me home, please." She left her art project on the table.

On the bus, she thought about Bernard. On top of it all, he had to do her the dishonor of dying first, twelve years ago now. And she had to watch, with gritted teeth, as her daughters immortalized him, writing songs for him, crying for him, mourning his pitiful legacy for months. It was a slow death, too, one that left him kinder and softer around the edges than he ever was as a healthy man. The bastard.

As much as she hated him, she still sometimes dreamed of him. She dreamed that he had found her, crawled to her on his knees, begging her: *What a fool, what a horrible, horrible monster I've been.* She would shut her doors to him, but he wouldn't stop. *Please, I'll do anything, please.* She would fall asleep to his banging fists, his singing of her name, *Estelle, Estelle, please, I'll die.* And then, eventually, she would have to let him in, because unlike him she was not cruel. She would have no choice but to accept his embrace. But even in the dream, he had cold hands, poor circulation from a weak heart. And when he'd touch her, the rude shock of the cold would jolt her back into her hatred again. She'd dreamt about him for so many decades, so many nights, that the fantasy became a memory, and she'd damn the bastard for even trying. How dare he, the fool.

At home, she checked her answering machine for messages from her daughters. There were none. Bernard never did try to get her back. He never looked behind as he walked out the door into the Puerto Rican heat. Never smiled at her from across the hospital room at their first granddaughter's birth or met her eyes from across the table at their daughters' weddings. It was as though she had nothing to do with them. He mocked her and taught her daughters how. He didn't give a damn about facts. He would tell stories to them at bedtime as they looked at him with dreamy, sleep-heavy eyes. All of it lies. His time in the military, his plan for their business, his stories about the ketchup during the Depression. He would hypnotize with lies. The papers tried their best not to lie. That's why she loved them. So much could be accomplished if people paid attention to the facts of things, and less to their emotions.

She ate her dinner alone, waiting for the phone to ring. She got one call from a telemarketer. She left a message for Julia, then Alma, then Susan. Maybe they were still working. They were always working late. As much as she longed to hear their voices, she was proud of them for that. Hard work, they learned that from her. After dinner, she lay in bed and began to read last Sunday's paper, an article about "minimalist living," a new thing people called being tidy and voluntarily poor. Her eyes grew tired at the thought of it. She folded the paper on top of a pile by her nightstand and switched off the light. As she did, she glided her palm over the newspapers' edges. A joy to have them there, eager to be read. She loved their gray, ink-blotted pages, folded like the wings of a sleeping pigeon. They held the answers to all of her questions, all of her aches and pains. If only she could sort them in such a way—a proper, neat, stylistically agreeable, non-hazardous way—that she could locate the precise articles when she needed them. But now she was falling asleep. Her last thought before the blue hushing shapes of a pleasant dream: she'd organize the papers in the morning.

About the author:

Originally from New York City, Lucy Marcus currently lives in Southwest Virginia where she is an MFA candidate at Hollins University. She also works as a facilitator for Global Nomads Group, where she connects high schoolers in the Middle East, North Africa, and the United States. Her fiction and poetry has appeared in 805 Lit+Art, First Class Lit, and The Grinnell Review.

RULES
©2018 by Rebecca Evans

At ten, I was already accustomed to the Boogeyman. Before bed, I'd clean the kitchen. This was one of my jobs. It was also a trap, a way for Daddy to get me in trouble. I'd stand in the center of my bedroom, waiting in the quiet, a signal that it was safe to go downstairs. Barefoot, I squeezed the shag with my toes until the basement door closed, my cue. The tiny yellow light over the stove dimly guided me from the stairs to the kitchen. My eyes adjusted, but I could perform the task blindfolded, if needed. As I stepped, the rips in the linoleum poked the tender underbelly of my feet. Green fridge, white and black stove, yellow dishwasher, chipped sink; all worn, second-hand and an indication of our poverty. I moved in a zigzag to avoid triggering the boards into a moan.

Soundlessly, I loaded the dishwasher, remembering to leave off the tap, the process slow, one dish at a time. I maintained space between each plate, deflecting any *clinks*. I kept the silence.

At the time, my room was scattered with a handful of Barbies and Nancy Drew books, a flashlight on my nightstand to read undercover, my cello leaning in one corner. Beneath my mattress was my stash of coloring books, hidden. Not because I'd be in trouble, but because I was embarrassed that I still enjoyed such a baby-like activity. I could lose myself in those shades. I controlled the depth of color-bleed onto the page solely with the pressure of my fingertips. Sometimes, I created make-believe stories in my sketches. The kind where the princess kills the dragon and burns him to ashes.

Sometimes I fell asleep. On accident. This was one of those times. A rap on my half-opened door (because I was not allowed to keep my door shut) had startled me awake. He stood in the doorway, filled the frame, legs wide, belly drooping over his jeans, hands on his hips. I can still see the outline of him, his long, black beard, the straggling hairs creating a dark halo near his ears.

"There's dishes downstairs," he said. Though I never knew him to drink, his words sounded slurred, especially at night.

This time, I had left on my light. It worked. I tricked him. Yet I knew I only fooled him once and tomorrow, I'd need to discover a different method to keep him at bay.

"Okay. Sorry," I said. I waited. He left and I was thankful I remembered another rule: never brush against him to squeeze through the doorway. Body contact could stir him and I'd spend the night restraining my screams because he would only stop hurting me once I quieted. Once I stopped fighting. He'd quit when he was through, but it would end faster if I lay lifeless, unresponsive.

Back in the kitchen was a new mess. Another gimmick of his, indulging in a later snack. The rules always changed. Melted ice cream drizzled from the tipped bowl, from the counter to the floor. I sopped the puddle, cleaned the debris. As I departed, I offered the room a once over, glancing towards the table. Each chair was pushed away, a carefully laid ambush. They were too heavy to lift; instead I "walked" them, leg by leg, back to where they belonged.

As I settled into bed again, I realized I'd forgotten the weapon. I snuck back. Now it was after midnight and Mother was still away at one of her three jobs, waitressing. I listened at the top of the stairs. Once all was hushed, I rushed to the kitchen, opened the drawer, grabbed the knife. The big one. Returned to my room. Undetected. Placing it under my pillow was a new system, though I had forgotten to use it during the last time, stifled and stunned, incapable of protecting myself. I promised myself that I would remember. Promised I would use it next time.

I was never good at sustaining self-promises and I'm no longer ten. I'm over fifty and I think about how self-preservation at that young age shaped me today. As a mother. As a woman. I no longer sleep with a blade beneath my pillow, but I carry a can of mace. For a time, I kept a can of wasp spray near my bed because I read somewhere that it could reach an intruder at least twenty feet away. I check the locks, then I wake, and check them again. My childhood wasn't the only life-chapter that developed my over-cautionary tendencies. My military service and, later, an abusive marriage, heightened my anxiety. There's a balance. This is what I tell myself. There is also an acceptance. I find little harm holding an extra can of security at the end of the day. It is worth the peaceful sleep of my children, worth their blessed unawareness of the Boogeyman.

About the author:

Rebecca Evans served eight years in the United States Air Force, and is a decorated Gulf War veteran. She hosts the Our Voice television show, advocating personal stories, and mentors teens in the juvenile system. She held the title of Mrs. Idaho International and earned a B.A. in Creative Writing from Boise State University, minoring in Psychology, and was also honored with the BSU "Women Making History in Idaho" award. Her work has appeared in Gravel Literary magazine and is forthcoming in Fiction Southeast. She's currently pursuing an MFA in Creative Writing at Sierra Nevada College and serves on the editorial staff of the Sierra Nevada Review. She lives in Idaho with her three sons.

LAP DANCE
©2018 by Jennifer Companik

He told himself he could drink a beer and watch the women—that he didn't really have to touch anyone. He also held fast to the idea that customers weren't allowed to touch the girls in such places and that the girls probably didn't want to touch the customers very much, anyway, so he'd be safe. Gabe wore thick glasses. His aversion to haircuts showed in the way his black hair hung from his scalp like a neglected pelt. Depending on whether he'd been feeding his depression or starving it, his clothes were either too tight or too loose. And he was shy. Gabe had never been purposely fondled by a sober woman he did not know.

He had not expected the wall of smoke he walked into after paying the five-dollar cover charge. Smoking indoors had been against the law in Arkansas since 2006. But then, Gabe wasn't there for his health. Between the smoke and the extremely dim lighting, he could barely see. Music engulfed him; music so loud, so vibratory Gabe felt aware of his appendix. He stood just inside the door for a minute while his eyes adjusted and his lungs stirred with longing: Gabe hadn't smoked in three years. Surely they sold cigarettes at Delilah's Cabaret.

When he could see, he looked around.

The middle of the room held a stage on which a spotlight pulsated in different colors, changing the scrawny blonde grinding on the pole from a Smurf to a Martian to a scarlet fever victim then back to blonde. He did not recognize the song, the lyrics of which amounted to a rhythmic recitation of racially insensitive terms.

He made out small round tables and a few sizable booths arranged in a circle around the stage. He would sit as far from the speakers as possible to keep his insides from quivering while he drank. There were other customers, none of whom made eye contact with him as he crossed the room.

What had @CynthiaGleans said that brought him to this shadowy room? @CynthiaGleans: He thought of her like that, by her handle—had even dreamed of her that way once—not of her scantily clad avi, just her handle. She'd said: "It can be nice, being touched by a stranger." It had made him wonder if, after months of chatting online, Cynthia was still a stranger to him. And were she not married, Gabe might have ensouled the fantasy that flew into his thoughts when she'd said the thing about touching a stranger. But Gabe was done with married women.

A busty, lime-green corseted waitress took his beer order.

"Where can I get a pack of cigarettes?" he asked.

"There's a vending machine outside the john," she said, pointing to the men's room.

He acquired a pack of Camels. Across the hall from the vending machine, a host of cigars lounged in an unattended, locked glass case. That was how they skirted the smoking ban: the club was also, technically, a tobacco shop, and thus exempt. Having no lighter, he lit a cigarette from the candle burning in a small red cup on his table.

Gabe took a closer look around. A different girl had mounted the stage; a brunette with cartoonishly large silicone-plated breasts. She wore a gold colored dress in a wet-looking fabric that blended almost perfectly with her skin, her face pretty but unsmiling.

He was looking for someone, on Cynthia's suggestion, who looked happy to be there—someone who caught his eye.

It had been a less jocular conversation, the one that brought him there, than he usually had with Cynthia. More personal than previous exchanges. Cynthia had written that her friend's dog, a "small, smelly, territorial animal," had persecuted her all week, chasing her around and licking her legs. She found dog saliva disgusting.

Knowing Cynthia seldom left her hometown for more than a day or two, seven days seemed like a long time for her to be away from home. He'd asked why she was staying at a friend's house.

"This friend lives far. I love her. Haven't seen her in over a year. Turns out I know her new poet-husband, too." She paused a minute then added, "She's an ex-lover, Gabe. So is he. I must've needed to hear them finish an English sonnet together this morning, at four o'clock. You know, to learn my heart still had a spot intact enough to break."

Gabe hadn't known what to say to such a revelation or what color to assign the sad, erotic image it evoked.

Later in the conversation she'd asked him why he disliked getting haircuts.

"I don't like being touched by strangers," Gabe had told her.

That was when, among other things, she'd said: "I was once mashed against a handsome stranger on a train for three stops. At one point we could have changed positions, but neither of us did. I was sad when we came to my stop."

"The exception may prove the rule," Gabe had said, his imagination tumid with the image of Cynthia and the stranger on the train.

She'd continued: "A woman on an airplane once handed me her red-haired baby so she could 'use the bathroom alone for the first time in a year. It was nice."

"Didn't the baby cry?" Gabe had asked.

"He didn't. He put his fingers all over my face and laughed: I almost died of happiness."

Gabe had never known anyone who'd died of happiness. He himself struggled, daily, for contentment. Gabe then thought of strangers who had touched him.

"When strangers touch me it's usually a hand shake. Mostly I shake hands with poor people who hardly ever shower."

"The people you help in your work."

"Yes. Sometimes people with track marks on their arms hug me." Occasions, Gabe had thought but not said, on which he struggled to avoid visibly recoiling.

"You've never had a massage?" she'd persisted.

"No." He had almost had a massage. He'd gone with a friend who had a two for one coupon at a spa, but left when he learned he'd have to take all his clothes off.

"Hasn't a doctor or nurse ever touched you in a gentle, healing way?"

"No. That's why I only go to the doctor when I think I might die if I don't. I'm much more comfortable," Gabe had said, stroking his German shepherd Trixie between the ears, "being licked by dogs."

The waitress brought his beer. He paid for it and over-tipped her. Gabe ate nothing but canned beans for up to a week between paychecks—social work paid just enough to keep the lights on—but when in a place where tipping was expected, he over-tipped. He'd learned, through many cans of beans, to avoid such places. But tomorrow was payday and he'd just sold a painting for three-hundred and sixty-five dollars. Gabe smoked with a feeling like satisfaction: he felt rich.

Did anyone look happy to be working there? What kind of woman would find such work fulfilling?

Cynthia had been a stripper in college.

"For the most part, I liked giving lap dances," she'd said. "I'm an affectionate person. Actually, if I've ever had a problem touching people, it's been me touching people a little too much. I come from a very affectionate family: I had to learn not to touch everyone."

Gabe had wondered what that was like.

"I'm probably not an affectionate person," he'd told her. "But

I've never had a lap dance; you're making me feel like maybe I'm missing out on something. I could choose the stranger who'd be touching me in a lap dance."

"You should do it!" Cynthia'd said.

"Maybe."

"You totally should. I want to hear all about it."

A woman dressed like a mermaid smiled at Gabe from several tables over. She had been sitting with a customer, her back to him, when he walked in. Her hair looked real. She had honest-to-god mermaid-type hair. Hair into which he fantasized for a moment about burying his face. And her smile seemed friendly. A handful of other women had met his eyes briefly and smiled but their smiles had felt, if anything, vaguely hostile. Halfway through his beer he noticed the other men in the room wore business suits. Him? He only felt rich: In his worn sneakers and button-down flannel shirt, Gabe realized he looked to these women like a can of beans.

He extinguished his cigarette.

The mermaid stood up and walked out of the room, in the opposite direction of his table, just as another girl sat in the chair next to his.

He was down to his last swig of beer. He could leave.

He didn't leave.

He wondered what the girl would be like. Why she picked his table. If maybe she was an affectionate person. If, like Cynthia suggested, strippers offered, besides entertainment, comfort to lonely men. If such a thing were even possible.

He closed his eyes.

Gabe avoided asking himself if he was lonely. He worked, he painted, he saw his friends, he played with his dog. He sometimes asked himself if he'd be happier with a woman in his life. It was not a simple question for Gabe.

At thirty-four Gabe lived alone. Most of his friends had married. Some had kids. Thinking about marriage made Gabe's stomach ache. There had been, for three years, a woman—an unhappily married woman—he would have married. And though Gabe liked the idea of kids, he felt it would be stupid—even if by chance a qualified, willing, single woman appeared—to bring children into his penury. Gabe worked with the children of penury. It depressed him.

He hardly noticed he'd closed his eyes—to the smoke, the lights, and his solitude. Gabe was an artist. He collected images and picked out colors and symbols for his paintings. Gabe knew he loved painting more than he could love any woman. Interacting with the person beside him might prove artistically fruitful—but not with his eyes closed.

She hadn't moved.

She smelled strongly of cinnamon. Gabe disliked the smell of cinnamon. He tried to put her scent out of his mind. It wasn't her fault he hated the smell of cinnamon—that it was something the sour grandmother who half-raised him sprinkled on everything including french fries. How could this kindly stripper girl know he associated the smell of cinnamon with his mother abandoning him when he was eleven? And while he was here broadening his experience of life and collecting images, might he not at least try to let this girl redefine the smell for him?

"I'm Diamond," she said, extending a small, white-gloved hand.

"Gabriel." They shook hands. He felt sweaty though the room was cold. He worried he'd sweat onto her glove, so he pulled his hand away quickly.

He'd have to look at her face. He needed another beer. He waved to the waitress, holding up his empty beer bottle, signaling for another.

"I've never seen you here before," Diamond said.

A tarantula he worried he could only wash down with a few more beers stood in his throat.

"Are you having a good night?" Diamond asked.

Politeness compelled Gabe to look at her, so he did. "I'm shy," he croaked.

"Me, too," she said.

The waitress brought his second beer. He paid.

Diamond looked very young. Like she should be on a study date with a boy her age who should have to wait a few dates before he got to see her naked. She had acne on her forehead and chin that no amount of makeup could conceal. She'd gathered her short, light brown hair in red barrettes on either side of her face. The redness of her lipstick in contrast to the paleness of her skin gave her the air of a naked mime. She wasn't naked, per se, but her red and white striped dress had a huge cutout in the midsection and only barely covered her elsewhere. Looking at the quantity of breast spilling from the top of her dress made Gabe shift in his seat: it felt wrong to be sexually attracted to someone so much younger.

He drank half the second beer in one gulp.

"How can you be shy and do this job?"

"There's not really a lot of talking," she said.

"What about the other stuff?"

"I'm high."

"Oh."

He gulped down the rest of his beer.

He could leave. He could fake going to the bathroom and never come back. He thought about the possibility of touching Diamond and stood.

"I'm not pretty," she said, "but I have really nice tits. If you wanna see them, it's thirty-five dollars."

He hesitated.

"Please, Gabriel. I haven't made much money this week and rent is due tomorrow."

Gabe sat down.

"What happens in a lap dance?"

"I dance on your lap, put my tits in your face."

He made the mistake of allowing his eyes a dip into her cleavage. It had been a while—pictures aside—since he'd seen a woman's naked breasts.

"Okay," he said, telling himself he was helping the girl pay her rent.

Gabe followed Diamond through a short hallway into an even darker room. The only light came from the candles on the tables, tables smaller than the ones near the stage and set beside leather couches behind translucent room dividers. Whispers and some laughter emanated from the couches. He could still hear the music, but at this distance it did not shake his pancreas.

Diamond found an empty couch where she bade him sit next to her "Until the next song starts so you get a full dance." Gabe sat next to her. His right forearm was touching her left arm. He felt clammy, she felt warm. He noted the gentle pressure of her outer thigh against his. A waitress brought a beer he had not ordered but for which he was, nonetheless, grateful. He took a long swallow. The beer, very cold, cleared the tarantula from his throat.

When a new song started, Diamond popped up off the couch, slid her dress down her hips, and straddled him. His arms moved, reflexively, to encircle her waist, but he withdrew in the last second. He did not want to get his fingers broken by whoever broke fingers in this place.

Cynthia had told him a story about a man who'd tried to stick his finger in her vagina during a lap dance and how she'd screamed and how a bouncer named Tommy had emerged from a nearby shadow and in the scuffle that ensued, broken four fingers of the offender's right hand. Gabe's outrage on Cynthia's behalf had traveled through time, beginning the night of the attempted assault, and was only partly assuaged by the Hammurabian punishment. That Tommy broke the man's fingers had been just. But justice might prove fickle in a place like Delilah's. Gabe shuddered.

"You can touch me above the waist. If you want," Diamond said, rubbing her large, exquisite breasts against his face.

Gabe sat on his hands. He would not touch her. She could touch him, if she chose.

Diamond danced sinuously against him. She felt good in the

dark.

He couldn't smell her perfume anymore or had gotten used to it. His body stirred. If he bought another dance, she'd stay where she was.

"No biting or scratching, though," she added.

"What?"

"No biting or scratching," she repeated.

Who on earth had bitten this girl? Or scratched her? How had he become someone she needed to say that to?

"Would you please put your dress back on," he said, pulling his face as far as he could from her very near breasts.

Diamond burst into tears.

"What's wrong? Did I hurt you?" He asked, panicked both by her tears and by the possibility of encountering this club's Tommy.

Some of her tears fell on his face before she retreated from his lap.

"What's wrong with my dancing?" She asked, between hiccupping sobs. She sobbed for an entire verse.

"Do people really bite you and scratch you when you dance for them?" Gabe asked.

The tears stopped, but her chest still heaved. Diamond knelt beside him now, carefully avoiding touching him, using the mirror behind the couch to check her makeup.

"Are you buying another dance?" she asked, arms crossed, mouth tight, when she stood up. "I can't stay back here if you don't."

He pulled two twenties from his wallet and handed them to her.

She folded them into her garter and stared at him.

Gabe couldn't stand being stared at.

A new song snaked into the room; another unfamiliar song, the lyrics faint.

"I don't turn tricks," she said. "I'll dance for you, but that's it."

"Would you stay dressed and talk to me?"

"It costs the same."

"That's fine."

Diamond, still standing, shifted her weight from one foot to the other on white, patent-leather, five-inch stiletto heels. "Where should I sit?"

"Here," he said, patting the place beside him on the couch.

She sat, arms still crossed. "You could talk to a regular girl someplace else for free."

Gabe studied her face. Her pupils were huge in the dark. She had light brown eyes almost the same shade as her hair. She darkened her thin, straight eyebrows with pencil. She slouched such that her chin nearly touched her chest.

"You can tell me things another girl wouldn't know."

She raised her head, her eyebrows moving a bit higher on her forehead. "Like what?"

"Like why you were crying before."

She took off her left glove and pulled a cigarette from the tiny purse she carried. She lit her Newport with a candle. She took a drag and blew rings into the air before them.

"Why'd you ask me to get dressed?"

"The biting thing."

"If that's your thing, I know a girl here who likes that—"

"It made me sad."

"That I told you not to bite me? Jesus, you're sick."

"It made me sad that anyone would hurt you like that. That you thought I might hurt you."

"Oh."

"You do have really beautiful breasts."

The song ended. Diamond stood up, extending her gloved hand by way of goodbye.

Gabe put forty more dollars in her hand.

Diamond sat back down.

"You still haven't told me what made you cry."

Diamond finished her cigarette and dropped it, smoldering, into a nearby ashtray.

"I don't like talking."

Gabe considered leaving. He'd already spent more money than

he planned. He'd had his lap dance—or a fraction of one, anyway. He could tell Cynthia about the plain, temperamental girl with the lovely breasts who'd wept on him. He could tell it funny or he could tell it sad. He'd never heard Cynthia's voice, but he liked to imagine her laughter. He'd tell it funny. He could leave now and tell it funny.

He looked again at Diamond.

She started to laugh.

He remembered she was high. Maybe he'd been angsting over her tears when they were nothing more than a drug-induced mood swing?

"I'll buy one more song, if you tell me what made you cry. And why you're laughing now."

She giggled down, almost straightening her face, but then laughed again. Louder.

"Do we have a deal?"

"Sure."

"So?"

"What's funny is I've made more money in the last twenty minutes dressed than I normally make in three hours of taking my clothes off. I mean, know I'm not pretty, but you just *paid* me to keep my clothes on."

Gabe had not thought of it that way. But that she could laugh at the irony made him like her.

"They'll make fun of me when they find out."

"Who?"

"The other girls."

"Won't they just make fun of me? For being stupid?" Gabe asked.

"You, too, Gabriel. They'll make fun of both of us."

"I'd never bite or scratch you."

Diamond pulled a spaghetti strap off her shoulder and smiled. "We could talk while I dance for you."

He would paint the look on her face when she pulled her strap down. That was the image he'd needed.

Gabe sat back as she straddled him again.

"No one will break my fingers if I put my hands on your waist?"

"No one will break your fingers."

Gabe laid his hands gingerly on her waist.

Another song started. Gabe pulled more twenties from his pocket.

For one night, he could be rich.

About the author:

Jennifer Companik holds an M.A. from Northwestern University, reads fiction for *TriQuarterly*, and writes for *RadiantStreets.com*. Her accomplishments include: first-prize in *The Ledge*'s 2014 Fiction Awards Competition; 2016 Pushcart Award Nominee, *Border Crossing*; fiction in *The Evansville Review*, 2017 issue; and a story forthcoming in *The Bryant Literary Review*. By reading her work you are participating in one of her wildest dreams.

PUNISHMENT
©2018 by Ruth Moors D'Eredita

I'm not sure how much you already know. This is not something I'm proud of.

It was twelve years ago. There was a good kid, he was fourteen, two years younger than you are now. His name was Anthony Green.

I shot him, and he died.

I was a union electrician back then. Mom and I were separated. You were four years old.

I was not a great dad, and I was not a great adult. I'd bounced around for a while after you were born. I wanted to work, but I also wanted to drink. When the union job opened up, I took it. But I had no seniority, and the economy was bad. I'd go down to the union hall every day and check the job chart. Most days they didn't use me. I was barely making a living that year.

Mom held it all together for us. She'd get home from work and make dinner and play with you. She read you your books before bed. She folded the laundry and watched her shows on TV at night.

I mostly drank. I drank in the house, and when Mom gave me the eye, I drank in the backyard. I busted things up. I drove drunk.

Mom got sick of it. I knew I was on thin ice with her. It unnerved me, like something was coming and I didn't know what it was or how to get myself out of the way of it. She started looking at me with this sadness, and taking deep breaths.

"The breathing is how you tune me out," I told her.

"It's yoga breathing, Bobby," she said. "Everything isn't always about you."

One night I came in late, drunk, and could barely walk. I bumped hard into the dresser in our bedroom. Mom sat up in bed and told me not to come home like that anymore.

"I'm sick of the goddamned drinking," she said. "If you think you're going to pass out every night like your father, you're wrong." My father was a good guy, and he worked hard, but Mom was right, he drank. He drank in his chair in the living room every night until he passed out.

I didn't know when I was a kid that, your dad's an alcoholic, you're a sitting duck for it. I'm not excusing myself. I want you to know you have to be careful. If you remember anything from your Sweet Sixteen today, honey, remember that.

The next morning Mom took you to preschool, came back in the house, and threw me out. She told me to shape up. "Come get your things after work," she said.

I went to stay with Grandmom.

I'd stop drinking, and make it a week, a month, and that's when I knew I was in a battle. Even on the days I was working, when I didn't feel like I was going to puke, I felt off.

I worked HVAC on the convention center for a while, then they put me on the parking garage at the stadium. I couldn't concentrate for longer than a few minutes. I thought too far ahead. I panicked I'd never stay sober. Coffee went down like acid. I couldn't eat. I slipped and drank a few times. After a few beers, I felt better.

The day I shot Anthony, I'd been sober again for a few weeks. But I hadn't seen you in a month. Mom wasn't calling me back. I had the shakes. That morning, I was down at the union hall looking at the job board. One of the foremen, Mike Doherty, came up to me.

I'd never been on a job with Doherty before. He was an old-timer, and kind of cantankerous. He was next in line to run our local. It felt like a chance to me.

"You're with me today, Bob," he said. "Clock in and meet me out back."

What a shithole his truck was.

He says to me, "We have to look at Twenty-first and Lehigh."

Let me stop here and back up and say a couple things.

Number one, Philly has the oldest electrical grid in the country. We don't shoot power out to one spot, like with direct current. It's alternating, and there's a lot of places for the grid to crash, all that extra equipment to balance the current. And it had been raining. When it rains hard, underground equipment goes down. Every component has to be cleaned and tested before they'll send power out again. And North Philly is not at the top of anyone's list for fixing things when they go down.

Number two, my entire life, I avoided North Philly. Most white people did. Every day, we heard about shootings and carjacks and gangs. One year, my mom went completely ballistic because the city was going to bus North Philly kids to our school. And my dad, like with everything else in his life, was disappointed by North Philly. When he got home from the service, he went to pharmacy school at Temple University. He loved it up there, he loved Broad Street, he loved the neighborhood. He hated that it went downhill. He'd read an article in the paper and say, "I guess they'll knife you for a nickel up there now." He'd watch the evening news and say, "Jesus Christ, what did they do to Beirut? It looks like North Philly."

He never thought about why that happened out there, and I didn't either.

That was my frame of mind when Doherty told me to clock in. Before I got in his truck, I went out to mine and got my Beretta. I tucked it under my shirt.

I should have told Doherty I was on edge, but I was intimidated. Doherty was not the type of guy to chat. He was listening to the radio. The Phils were ten games out already, the second week of May. They'd lost three of the last four at home. I remember Doherty shaking his head and snapping off the radio like he couldn't take it anymore. We pulled up to a video store.

The store was in an old brick building with apartments upstairs. They'd been on auxiliary power for a few days. The guys who went up in the bucket to check the pole earlier said the transformer checked out fine. It was our job to go inside and check the panel boards.

A group of kids stood on the corner. Up in an apartment window, a woman looked at us. The entrance to the store was grimy and the front windows were caged over. I followed Doherty inside.

"Yeah, how you doing?" Doherty said to the guy behind the counter. "Here to check your electrical."

The guy pointed to the back room. I took my flashlight from my belt and turned it on.

We saw a hallway and door. Doherty opened the door, and in the dim light we saw a toilet and janitorial supplies. No panel board anywhere.

Doherty said, "Probably in the cellar."

"Want me to go ahead? See what I can see?"

I was trying to make a good impression with Doherty. I needed the income to prove myself to your mom. If a guy like Doherty liked you, you worked.

I started down the cellar.

I didn't make it three steps when I hear a commotion on the landing behind me.

I turned, and in the beam of my flashlight saw an animal hanging from Doherty's pant leg. Doherty cursed and kicked the wall and whatever it was fell off and ran past my boots into the cellar. We heard it hit water.

I got itchy all over.

"Jesus Christ," Doherty said. "How wet is it down there?"

I shined my light and we both saw water up to the second stair.

"Yeah, okay, no," Doherty said.

I followed him back into the store. The kids who were out on the corner when we arrived were standing inside now, joking around up front.

"Yeah, we didn't find anything," Doherty said to the guy behind the counter. "Someone will get back to you."

The store was narrow, and the kids faced us, standing shoulder to shoulder in a little semi-circle between us and the door.

"Excuse me, son," Doherty said to a big kid in the middle.

The kid didn't move.

"Excuse me, son," Doherty said again.

This time Doherty took a little quarter step and started in just slightly with his shoulder between the big kid and the one next to him. The kid on Doherty's left yielded a little, but the big one planted himself and lowered his chin at Doherty. Some alert shot up inside me and surged into my brain like a flare.

That fast, the big kid swung and knocked Doherty to the ground. I lunged to grab Doherty but he fell hard and one of the other kids jumped on top of him and starting pounding him. The guy at the counter shouted *"Hey hey hey!"*

I wanted to get my back against something. I doubted I could make it out to the truck, and I couldn't leave Doherty in there alone. The kids to the left of me were laughing. They were young. I just remember thinking *No no no.* I squared off at the kid in front of me, Anthony Green.

During the investigation, the guy at the counter told the detectives that he heard me say, *No dude, come on, dude.* He heard me say Doherty was an old man, tell your friends to leave him alone, you can have our money. *Call it a day, man.*

I don't remember talking to Anthony.

I remember Anthony's eyes. The excitement shining in them. Anthony's eyes were filled with that wonder little kids lose after a while. He was having fun. I can still see his sneakers and his pants. They were nice school uniform pants. He had a neat haircut, shaved up the side. I remember thinking he wasn't very big.

Anthony held out his hand and told me to give him my wallet. I looked down past his open palm. On the floor, the kids were going through Doherty's pockets. I was scared. I thought to reach inside my shirt and grab my Beretta. Instead, I saw myself put my wallet in Anthony's hand.

Anthony lifted his shirt and put my wallet in his waistband. Then he raised his fist like he was going to pop me, too, like his friend popped Doherty.

I reared back a little and Anthony's fist grazed my shoulder. I lost my balance and lurched backward. I tripped over Doherty's leg and landed on my back on the floor next to him. Doherty was gasping, struggling to get up. I tasted stomach acid in my mouth. I looked up and Anthony was straddling me, looking down at me. I grabbed inside my shirt for my Beretta and leaned up and fired it at him.

Anthony fell back. He was making high, gulping noises. Now Doherty was on his knees, patting himself frantically. He looked at me and saw the Beretta.

I got on my feet and knelt next to Anthony. Blood was pulsing from his neck. It was staining the floor between us. Doherty looked from the blood to me with wild eyes. He shouted, "Who told you to fucking carry on my fucking job!"

I spread my hands on Anthony's collarbone and pressed down with my palms. I thought soon we would hear sirens, and I knelt there, pressing down. Anthony's blood filled the spaces between my fingers and colored my hands up to the wrists.

"Help is coming. Help is coming, buddy," I told Anthony.

In that moment, all I wanted was for Anthony to live. Wanting that, being unable to bring him back, has crowded out everything else. Anthony alive was all I wanted in the moments after I shot him, and all I've wanted since. I have never been clearer about anything. What I want most in life is for Anthony Green to be alive.

I was still kneeling over him when the police got there. They took Anthony to the ER at Temple, and he died.

Anthony's mother gave a statement to the prosecutor. The day Anthony died, she'd allowed him to walk home from school for the first time. He hated taking the bus. His mother said Anthony would have had straight A's that semester, but he had a C in Spanish. She told him he could walk home with his friends when he got the C up to a B. So after every Spanish class, Anthony asked his teacher to figure his average. The day before I shot Anthony, he got an A on a quiz. That afternoon, he got off the bus, ran inside, showed his mother his B average.

The next day he walked home with his friends. On the way they all stopped at the video store to see the Nintendos.

Anthony's mother said, "My son is dead because they see us different. My son wasn't worth anything to the man who shot him."

I can never stop hearing what she said. Because when I shot Anthony, everyone assured me: you get jumped, all bets are off, you're justified. My lawyer said it and it turned out to be true. The witnesses did not help the prosecutor. The guy at the counter told how, before he ran out the back, he heard me plead with Anthony. The lady upstairs didn't hear anything. And none of the kids remembered what happened the same way. One of them was twelve years old. Two of them had priors. All but the little one had reefer. My lawyer punched holes in all their stories. I got what they call a judgment of acquittal. And here is what I could never say out loud, but I want to say to you.

Once I gave Anthony my wallet, I didn't have to shoot him. I could have stayed quiet down there on the floor. I know right from wrong. The detectives who interviewed me got it right. Anthony would have followed the rest of his friends out the door. I knew that to be true then. Reading his mother's statement didn't so much confirm this truth to me as repeat what I already knew was true. I killed Anthony in a moment of fear, but there was anger in me in that moment, too. My anger pulled the trigger. And I haven't been punished for that.

The day of the acquittal, I drove up to see Mom and you. In the driveway up at the house, there were leaves all over the pavement. I saw your scooter leaning against the front step. I stood there for a minute, looking at the doorbell I installed when Mom and I moved in. I rang it.

I heard you run for the door and wait there on the other side before opening it, just like Mom taught you. Then I heard Mom, and the door opened.

"Daddy!" you said. You were excited to see me.

I bent down to pick you up. "Hi, Peach," I said. You inspected my ear with your little fingers. I felt your breath on my cheek.

"Mommy, it's Daddy," you said, like a little reporter.

Mom looked at you and me and said, "We have gymnastics at four."

I said to her, "Can I talk to you?"

"Honey, go on, get ready for tumbling," Mom said to you. "Daddy will still be here when you come down."

I will never be the kind of person who thinks ahead to reassure my own kid like that. I put you down and Mom and I watched you run upstairs.

Mom said, "Well?"

"Donna, I just came from court. I came straight here to see you," I said.

"Are you drinking?"

"No."

Silence.

"The judge granted the acquittal."

"Well, you didn't do it on purpose. Jesus."

I wanted to touch her. I wanted to reach my arms around her and gather her in and put my face against her neck and close my eyes and bawl, right there. My mind was saying, I did do it on purpose.

Instead, I said, "I will do better."

"Bobby, spare me," she said. "And you're planning to do what about work?"

"They say I can go back. I don't know how much work I'll get, but I can go back. Probably have to do nights for a while."

"Nights, Bobby. Are you serious?"

I closed my eyes. I knew what she was going to say.

The union didn't have to do anything for me. The cost-cutting guy in the mayor's office said not only did the unions rip the city off on pricing, but were criminals, too. A couple union thugs killed an honor student who'd done nothing more than walk into a video store after school. Maybe, the mayor said, it was time for the city to re-open all the union contracts. Maybe it was time to start thinking about right-to-work laws. Make the city more competitive for business.

But Doherty dug in. He told us one big non-union building goes up, that's like Stage 1 cancer. You throw everything you got at it, try to cure it. Two go up, it's Stage 2. You don't want it to get any worse. You hit the open job sites—the non-union sites—in the middle of the night and tear them up. Doherty's guys could destroy hundreds of thousands of dollars in concrete and steel and equipment and labor in half an hour.

Mom knew what was what.

"First off," she said, "nights is the worst thing you can do. They'll take advantage of you now. They'll have you out there busting up sites in the middle of the night, like you see in the paper. And for what? You get acquitted, and now you're going to go bust up scab sites for them? You going to prison for them after all? What are you thinking?"

"Not all night work is like that," I said. "There's good third shift work too."

She rolled her eyes at me. You know your mom. Her big thing is, actions speak louder than words. I had not even got to what I came to tell her.

So I said, "I want to live here with you and Kayleigh again."

Just then you came running down the steps in your gymnastics outfit and handed Mom your pink hairband. In two seconds, Mom put your hair in that ponytail like a little waterfall down your back.

I said, "Give me another chance, Donna."

I said it so low, I hardly heard it myself. But I said it.

"We have to go," she said.

I walked you out to the car and strapped you in your seat. I watched you and Mom drive up the street and turn onto the avenue. I got in my truck and drove back downtown.

Inside the union hall, guys were reading the paper and drinking coffee. I went into the back office. Doherty's door was open.

"Bob," he said, "What can I do for you?"

He did not stand up or even look at me full on.

"Hey, Mike," I said. "Thanks for taking me back."

"Them's the rules. So what can I do you for," he says again.

"Have anything you could put me on?"

Silence.

I tried again. "I'm trying to patch things up with my wife. I have to work."

As soon as I heard my words in the air between us, I thought about what Mom said when she kicked me out. Not everything is about me.

I tried to rephrase.

"You can count on me, Mike. I'm sorry about what happened."

"When you available?"

"Now."

"Third shift?"

"Sure," I said.

"Might have something for you in South Jersey."

"Thanks, Mike."

"Don't thank me. See Dave Joyce."

"Thank you," I said anyway.

At the pay window, Doherty's secretary handed me a slip of paper with Dave Joyce's number. I called him and he told me third shift on a cold storage warehouse job started at ten, he'd meet me there.

I drove east over the bridge across the Delaware. On the Jersey side, I filled up the truck at a Quik Stop and got a sandwich. At a picnic table in the parking lot, I ate and watched the planes take off at the airport. The sun set behind the oil tanks on the Pennsy side. I got back in my truck and slept for a while.

Then I drove out to the job site to be on time for Dave Joyce.

When I got out there, the site was at the edge of the Pine Barrens. I could see they'd cleared acreage for a warehouse. It's always so dark out there. There was no temporary lighting up yet, and a lot of the time, I installed the temp lighting. So I started getting my tools out of the back of my truck. If there'd been a second shift on that job, it was gone. In my headlights, I saw they had the concrete pad done, and were starting to frame.

I turned off my truck. Soon Dave Joyce showed up. He flipped on his headlamp so we could see. He had his belt on. He had an eight-pound sledge in one hand and his toolbox in the other.

He looked me over and said, "Ready? Follow me."

I walked behind him across an apron of surge gravel. He reached the chain link security barrier first. In the light of his headlamp, I saw the contractor's signage. It was an open site. There was no union on the job, and there was no third shift. Someone left the fork latch unlocked for us. I never found out who. Dave Joyce lifted it and we walked through the gate.

I followed him to the edge of the concrete pad and tried to swallow the fullness in my throat. I watched Dave Joyce line himself up to where the first, newly installed anchor bolt entered its steel column. He hoisted the sledge like a baseball bat, swung low at the bolt, and smashed it. The new-cured concrete cracked all around. The steel column it held in place rang and vibrated and gave way. The column tilted away from its base and took the concrete with it. Like when a tree falls and pulls up its root ball.

The half-circle of dark, piney woods around us absorbed the sound like it was nothing.

"Now do the rest of them," Dave Joyce said, and handed me the sledge.

About the author:

Ruth is from Philadelphia and lives and works in Vienna, Virginia, with her husband and three children. She is a member of the Woodbridge and Stafford workshops and is writing her first novel. "Punishment" is her first published story.

SUMMER MEMORIES
©2018 by Dorothy Robey

Ben Carleton carried his glass of iced tea, with just a sprinkle of sugar, to his front porch and seated himself in his rocker. Clouds blotted the blue sky and veiled the sun. The smell of freshly mowed grass hung in the dense air. Well-kept houses lined both sides of the street boasting immaculate lawns, four of which were being showered by sprinklers. Children gathered in the street, and then darted down the sidewalk in front of the sprinklers, drenching their clothes and hair. Giggles and shrieks followed.

Ben snorted. School wouldn't start for another two weeks. He sighed and counted ten kids. One of the boys, who looked to be around eight years old, closely resembled his Robert. *Where is Robert? Must be at a friend's house.* Ben nodded and took a sip of his cold beverage.

A tan station wagon rolled slowly down the street and came to a stop in front of his house. Four people emerged from the vehicle and strolled up the concrete path to his porch. The man had shoulder length, brown wavy hair, a clean-shaven face, and wore a button up short-sleeved shirt and shorts. Straight, long blonde hair hung on the woman with a thin, petite frame adorned in jeans and a t-shirt. Ben's face lit up. *Leo and his brood were coming today?* He shook his head, and the wrinkles in his forehead increased as his eyebrows came together. *The days get jumbled now that I've got time off work.*

"Hi." Leo waved and looked up. "It's going to be a scorcher

today."

"Yeah." Ben nodded.

July fourth at the family picnic. Yeah, that's when we got together last. His eyes scanned the street and houses. *A bunch of the neighbors joined the party. Debbie's daughter nearly burned her mitts on a sparkler.* He chuckled softly, and a productive cough followed. He pulled out a handkerchief from his pants pocket and wiped his nose and mouth, then shoved it back in the pocket.

Leo's two kids ran across the yard to join the other children. Leo and his wife sat down on the porch swing, smiling at Ben. He smiled back and sipped his tea again.

"David and Sarah are making the most of their last days of summer vacation," the woman said. She turned her blonde head in the direction of the cluster of kids now gathered on the lawn adjacent to Ben's.

"The office's AC went out Friday, and we all went home after lunch. It was too hot to stay sweltering in that box." Leo snickered.

People are so spoiled nowadays with air conditioning. Ben licked his lips and squinted at the sky.

Leo rose and pointed at Ben's glass. "Do you mind if I get some of that?"

"No. It's in the kitchen."

"Yeah, I know." Leo patted him on the shoulder.

Ben's gaze traveled to the blonde on the swing. She sat upright with her hands in her lap, the edges of her mouth turned upward. He sensed tension in the air but ignored it.

"Bob got two weeks off for our annual camping trip in the mountains." She wiped her damp forehead.

Ben shifted in his rocker. *Oh, yeah...forgot some folks call the kid brother by his middle name.* He scratched his prickly cheek. "Sounds nice. If only Barnestown had mountains. It's too damn flat."

She giggled.

The screen door opened with a squeak, and Leo stepped onto

the porch with two glasses in his hands. He gave one to his wife.

"It's one of my best batches," Ben crowed.

Leo took a long swig and smacked his lips. "Ahhh. I think that *is* your best yet."

Ben's eyes twinkled.

"Carol got promoted to supervisor at the shop," Leo said.

"Congratulations." Ben brought up his glass in a gesture of acknowledgement.

He eyed them as they spoke in low voices—too low—for Ben to hear. *Man and wife secrets.* Ben focused on the street where another car stopped in front of the house—a red sedan. Its grumbling engine died, and the driver's side door opened. A woman with chestnut hair pulled up in a bun, dressed in a white, knee-length dress, and large, round sunglasses, emerged from the vehicle and walked up the path.

Mary. Ben eased himself up from his rocker, his heart fluttering. *She's finally home.* His brows knitted. *Where the devil has she been?*

The kids screamed, chasing each other around the yard and into the street. A ball surfaced, and they kicked it around.

Mary approached the porch, removing her sunglasses.

"Mary, where've you been? At the store?" Ben wiped sweat from above his upper lip.

"No. I was at work." Mary smiled sweetly.

Ben lowered himself back into his rocker, as confusion etched in his weathered face. Mary, Leo, and his wife conversed in whispers. Ben squinted at them. *What's so big a secret they can't tell me?* He scratched his bristly chin and frowned. *Forgot to shave. Never missed a day in fatigues. But the war's over, and a man can grow a blasted beard if he wants to.*

"You planning the next atomic bomb?" he snorted and eyed the trio again.

Leo chuckled. "No. The first atomic bomb was enough."

"How are you feeling today?" Mary asked, walking toward Ben.

"I'm fine now that you're here." He gave her a wink and

grinned.

Mary laughed. "I'm going inside to check your medicines." She opened the screen door and disappeared into the house.

Ben grunted. *When are they leaving?* "Mary, when's Robert coming home?" he hollered in the direction of the front door. It brought on another short coughing jag.

Leo helped his wife out of the swing. "We'll be back in a minute."

They went inside his house with the glasses of tea.

They're leaving. I can feel it.

The kids were screaming again, as a car rumbled down the street. Its brakes squealed just before the sickening sound of it smashing into one of the children in the street.

"Oh, my God!" The screen door flew open as Leo's wife came streaking across the porch and down the two steps toward the group of kids now surrounding the child who had been hit.

The driver scrambled out of his car and hustled toward the knot of children. Leo rushed out of the house, followed by Mary.

Ben stood, his bones crackling and his muscles aching. *Did the war mess me up that badly? The kid needs help, and my damn legs are blasted lead weights.*

A handful of women came out of houses, mouths gaping.

"Call an ambulance!" one said.

Another ran back into her home.

Seven minutes later, sirens blared, and the ambulance parked in the street.

Damn it! Ben gritted his teeth and made his way down the steps, determined to be with the others.

The paramedics were strapping the boy on the stretcher when Ben arrived.

"Robert?" Ben caught his breath.

The boy's eyes were closed, his clothes rumpled, and bruises and blood splotches covered his face and body. Everyone around him talked simultaneously, frantic.

"Step back!" one of the paramedics said.

The majority of the children backed away—some returning to the yard next to Ben's. Two children remained close by Leo, his wife, and Mary.

Ben drew nearer. He caught another glimpse of the boy on the stretcher. "Robert!" he yelled in a hoarse voice.

He tried to push ahead of Leo and the others, but they took hold of his arms and stopped him. Panic filled his chest. He turned toward Mary. "Mary, that's Robert! For God's sake, do something!" He shook his arm, trying to loosen her grip. "Why the hell are you holding me back?"

"Come on back to your porch," Mary cooed.

She and Leo guided him back up the two steps. The boy was already inside the ambulance, and the paramedics were climbing into the front seat of the vehicle. Ben squeezed his eyes shut. *What about Robert?* The sirens squealed again and soon faded.

Mary helped Ben into his chair, his body wrought with achiness, his heart beating too fast, and his mind in turmoil. He scrubbed his perspiring face, as helplessness washed over him. "Why didn't we follow Robert?"

"I'm going to get your medication. You're due for it now. It's noon," Mary said.

"You're not going to answer me?" Exhaustion eroded Ben's frustration.

Leaning back in the rocking chair, he let out a long sigh.

Standing by the steps, Leo wore a pained expression, drew near to Ben, and knelt down in front of him. "It wasn't Robert. It was a kid named Jimmy. He lives two doors down from you. I think he'll be okay."

"Jimmy," Ben repeated the name in wonder.

Leo squeezed Ben's hand. Ben's brown eyes met Leo's soft, hazel ones.

"Where's Robert?"

"Dad, I am Robert."

About the author:

Dorothy has been writing since her pre-teen years. In her early twenties, she became a member of the Rocky Mountain Writer's Guild in Denver, Colorado, from 1993 to 1995. Between 1997 and 2014, she spent those years as a stay-at-home mom to her two sons. She is currently a third-year undergraduate student majoring in English Creative Writing online at Southern New Hampshire University and has written several short stories, one novel, and two short plays. One of those short plays called "Falling Up Stairs" was performed on stage at a local theater in York, Pennsylvania, on January 20, 2018. Dorothy lives with her family in Lancaster, Pennsylvania.

DRENCHED
©2018 by Israela Margalit

She looked for a large umbrella. A small one could bend in the wind. A big one could bend in the wind. Water was desperately needed and a steady soft rain that quenched the soil would have been ideal. Instead, there was a downpour for the ages. And all this on the same night he came to see her after years. He called to say he was in town. This implied he lived elsewhere but she didn't ask. She didn't ask how he had found her cell phone number, either. She didn't ask the purpose of his visit, or what he expected from contacting her—if indeed he had expectations. A surge of pride overcame her, as though she'd passed a crucial life-exam with high marks.

"Oh, hi. Nice to hear from you," she said.

She could hear him chuckle ever so slightly, pleased with her greeting, or concealing discomfort. She remembered well the sound of it from years past, always baffling her with its ambiguity.

"How are you?"

Other people asked the same question, not so much a question as a conduit to the rest of the conversation: how are you, can you come to my reading, how about lunch on Wednesday? In Oliver's mouth the question was personal, fraught with meanings that reverberated long after the words had been spoken. How are you, *I wish we could take a walk in the park right now.* How are you, *I miss you.* How are you, *I want to live with you inside the hole of a needle.*

How are you?

Her pulse quickened. "I'm well. Great actually. Working, writing. And you?"

"Same, basically. I have a new book in galleys."

"Congratulations. I'd be happy to read it."

"Of course."

"What's the title?"

"I think it would surprise you."

"Very little can surprise me."

As soon as she uttered the words she bit her lip. The hardness of her scar tissue had been carefully hidden, not exposed to anyone, not even Ben. She relaxed her tone of voice. "Though I have no doubt your title *will* surprise me. You have the gift of originality."

He didn't answer. She hoped that he was lingering over her praise rather than mulling over the hostility of her earlier comment.

"I'm more concerned about having something to say of enduring value," he said with a chuckle. "Thank you, though. I'll get you a copy."

She breathed a sigh of relief. In years past, his imperviousness had caused her pain, but right now it made her feel safe. They were in familiar territory: she divulging her frustration, he oblivious to her mood, or feigning to be. She had to end the conversation without another incident.

"I'll read it with great pleasure."

"Means a lot."

"Goes without saying."

"I don't believe you read my last book."

"Is this your third?"

"I sent you...you were on the list."

"We moved twice."

There was a hush, the gulf of the years with their load of secrets between them.

"It would be best to send the new book to me at school," she said.

"Will do. Though...can I see you?"

Sorry, I don't think it's a good idea. I'm terribly busy. I really don't want to go there. She was ready for that moment, having rehearsed it in her mind over and over again even though there was nothing to suggest it was coming. But the instant he asked she knew she desperately wanted to see him. She had to.

"Meet me on the street corner at seven."

The stillness that followed was ominous.

"Which street corner?" he asked.

"Eighty-second and Columbus."

He burst out laughing, his unadulterated joy sucking the magic out of the moment. She wished she could retreat into her earlier cautious self, before she had said those fateful words.

"What's amusing?" she asked.

"The first time I attended your class, you critiqued a student for using an address in his story. You said trivia was the enemy of the interior monologue. Trust the reader to fill the gap."

"I was right," she said. "'Meet me on the street corner at seven' would have been just perfect."

He laughed softly, and she laughed with him, their voices mingling. Intimacy restored, she wanted to say more, but he had already hung up. As always, he didn't claim the last word, but he took command of the last beat of silence.

The sun was shining when he called and she was not aware that it would be raining madly only a few hours later, though the forecast was sixty percent showers. But even disregarding the elements she could have told him to meet her in her apartment. He'd have time to come over at seven, have a glass of wine, and leave before Ben got back from work. Ben was never at home before eight, and tonight he had a staff meeting so he'd be even later. Or she could have invited him for a drink at seven, and he could have stayed for dinner with her and Ben like reemerging old friends sometimes do.

She found a large black umbrella. The black umbrella would make her look older. She *was* older. It was the only wide umbrella she could find, apart from a dusty oversized green Wimbledon umbrella—a relic from her youth when she and Ben used to wait for hours in the unrelenting London rain for the first ball to be played, doing the wave with a crowd of people who had likewise stood in line for half the night. She and Ben shared a love of tennis, a love of literature, a love of each other.

She shoved both large umbrellas, the black and the green, into the back of the closet. She'd go out with her elegant polka-dotted small umbrella, the one that shed warm light on her complexion and made her look like she still had potential. As a woman, that is. As a writer she had given up long ago. Her early novels probed the lives of people who struggled to survive under the social radar, whose chance of moving up the ladder was practically nonexistent. Those novels were received well enough to earn her a tenured professorship, but—just like their protagonists—didn't go further, selling a few copies, then disappearing quickly from the shelves. Then came a novel saturated with her unbridled anguish, a story of a man who had withered a woman's heart like the drought did the land. It instantly climbed to the top of the chart. Even though it was a piece of fiction, so much of it had been lifted from her clandestine experience, she felt guilty of plagiarism. After the buzz had died down she was grateful not to have been found out, but fell into depression worse than the one that spawned the writing of the novel. She had nothing more to say and no desire to say it. Feeling calm became her goal. A good day was a day when she felt content viewing the world through the holes of the net that kept her together.

She put on some more makeup to the sound of rolling thunder. She could still call him to cancel. His number was on her cellphone like all incoming callers except for those unidentified. He was identified. A New York number. She wondered why he had a New York number if he lived elsewhere: did he come to town often enough to have a local phone? Was he in a relationship, in love, in agony—she stopped mid-thought, alarmed by how quickly she'd rushed into her obsessive whirlpool of yore. It would be prudent to postpone the meeting until she was ready, or better: until she grew so old that time had stripped her memories of their poignancy.

"Oliver? Why didn't you come last night? I waited for an hour. Has anything happened? Did you get into an accident? I'm so worried. Can you give a sign of life?"

"Oliver, I know you said... But you wouldn't just break it off without a last goodbye? When can we meet?"

"Oliver, how can you be so cruel? I know you're not sick. Someone told me you gave a brilliant lecture in Los Angeles. What were you doing on the west coast? When are you coming back? *Are* you coming back?"

"Oliver, are you at home? Wrong number?"

Years ago she swore to never again call him no matter the excuse, a decision as essential to her survival as the choice to take the next breath. It took years before not calling him became as natural a part of her life as calling him had been before. She couldn't carelessly break that pledge, like an alcoholic taking just that one sip, even as she could easily convince herself that calling him now was not like calling him then, that she was a different woman, that she was free.

She *was* free, so much so that it took her a few seconds to identify his voice on the phone. True, the tone of his voice had never affected her as acutely as the shape of his arm, or the odor of his sweatshirt after jogging, and yet, fervor such as hers should have left a mechanism of instant recognition, at any skin-to-skin touch, any spoken word. That it did not was more reassuring than she could have hoped for. Maybe she had achieved more distance from her past than she'd given herself credit for. Maybe seeing him would help her find closure, or at least an explanation: why he had been there to begin with, why he abruptly left, what had happened in between. There were other questions on her mind, but she was aware the answer might throw her entire existence out of kilter. The ache of knowing he had not loved her, then departed once there was nothing left to seduce, would be unbearable. The ache of knowing their relationship had been too insignificant for him to even probe the depth of his attachment would be unbearable. There was only one answer that could pacify her insatiable heart— a confession of his eternal longing—but even that would be unbearable because it would threaten to obliterate everything that she called her life.

Despite the intensity of their relationship, she couldn't recall the nuances of his features. She remembered his dirty blond hair parted to the left that often fell over one eye. That and the smile on his face when he first read his poem to her. That smile was carved under the outer layer of her skin where it could not be removed without killing her. His smile implied a shared secret though his eyes were downcast, looking into himself. At the time she interpreted it as shyness. Later she wondered whether already then he was playing the game he was so apt at, but she dismissed the thought. She was willing to trash every other bit of recollection for the sake of her peace of mind, but not those first precious encounters.

"I've written a poem. It's not good, but it's the only one I have."

"Maybe it's better than you think."

"I was excited about it at first, but then I realized that I was just thrilled about writing something from start to finish. I feel like an amateur."

"The distance between amateurs and professionals is breached by studies, hard work, and a healthy dose of self-doubt."

"I have plenty of the latter," he said with a chuckle.

She stopped to look at him, enchanted by his sincerity. There was a rhythm to their conversation that made her feel light on her feet.

"Good. Now we're getting somewhere."

There was a row of students waiting to talk to her.

"Come to open reading tomorrow and let us hear your poem."

"I'd be crushed if you rejected it."

"You may not have to cross that bridge, so why suffer now?"

"It's easier to fail if you're prepared for it."

"No, it isn't," she said.

He chuckled and ceded his place at the front of the line.

She forgot that conversation until the next day, when he read his poem in class. It was not a love poem, and yet the fragility of his images made it penetrate through her pores as if it were. She remembered distinctly the poem's first dozen words, to which she listened with her capacity for critical analysis intact. Then she got lost in the indefinable, unsure if it was the poem that touched her so deeply or his elusive smile that implied, I wrote it for *you*. She fumbled in her bag for something that could help stabilize her for a moment, though it was too late. She was inside his poem, her certainty vanished.

When he finished reading he raised the curtains over his anxious eyes, the emotion between them palpable: Is my poem good? Is my poem good enough to get me admitted? Is my poem good enough to get me a scholarship? Is my poem good enough to get published in your journal?

Is my poem good enough to make you sleep with me?

It was half past six. She sat down to write a note to Ben. Several notes.

A drink with an old friend. Back soon.

Singing in the rain. See you later.

Out to a movie. Dinner on the stove.

If I'm not back by midnight you'll know I didn't deserve you. I never have.

She tore them into pieces. She'd call Ben later, when she knew what she was doing. All sort of scenarios were racing through her head.

She'd be waiting on the street corner for ten minutes and Oliver wouldn't show, like he didn't for their last rendezvous.

She'd step out onto the empty street looking for a slender man with an umbrella, but instead a black car would stop for her and he'd whisk her in.

She'd wave to him, and he'd get so excited, he'd drop his umbrella and rush from the corner for a never-ending embrace.

She'd step out to the street and see him at the corner, his arm around the shoulder of a woman whom he'd introduce as his wife.

She'd walk toward him and he'd say he'd been offered her job, and he felt that after all she had done for his career he should tell her in person.

She'd walk toward him and gaze at his emaciated pale face, and he'd say he had only a few weeks left to live and he wanted to say goodbye.

She'd walk toward him and say hello. "You haven't changed much." She couldn't be that banal. "It's been a long time." She couldn't be that sentimental.

"I forgot your face." That was more likely. Aggressive but true.

I forgot your face. I forgot your voice. I can't forget the hours of the days that seemed hollow when you weren't around.

She put on her raincoat and buckled the belt a notch tighter than she usually did. She opened and closed her tiny umbrella to make sure it worked. She grabbed her bag and checked her phone for a last-minute text message. It was five minutes to seven. She stepped out of the apartment and headed to the elevator. It was waiting on the first floor. She pushed the button. It flickered. The other day a neighbor got trapped inside for an hour. She couldn't take a chance. She started to walk down the stairs. She didn't run because the last time she did—*they* did, she and Ben—he tripped and broke both his legs. She walked down cautiously, slowly leaving behind floor after floor. When she had nearly reached the bottom, she heard a sequence of sounds in orderly succession as on a movie track: a door opening, steps on a stone floor, umbrella shaking in the air, spraying water, a man coughing—Ben. He looked at her, surprised.

"Going out in this weather?"

"I'm running to the drugstore. Aren't you early?"

"The meeting got cancelled. We sent everybody home."

He tried to close his umbrella. "It's raining buckets. I just bumped into Oliver outside. Dripping water."

"Oliver the poet?"

"In the flesh. Haven't seen him in forever. He hasn't changed much."

He looked at the elevator. It was waiting on the fourth floor. He pushed the button. It flickered.

"They should really fix this thing," he said.

She smiled.

"I know what you're thinking," he said.

"What?"

"That I should walk up the stairs. I know. I've got to start exercising."

"You sure do," she said.

"I'll join your gym next week," he said. "I promise."

He pushed the button again. It flickered.

"Did Oliver say what he was doing in town?" she asked.

"I invited him upstairs to dry off and have a drink but he said he was already late for something."

"It's impossible to be on time on a night like this," she said.

"My words exactly, but he said he was twelve years late."

She felt her heart skip a beat. He shook his umbrella again. Bits of water splattered around. He removed a drop of water from her cheek. "You look pretty with your makeup on."

She smiled. He smiled back. "I wonder what it means, being twelve years late for a meeting. Twelve years is an eternity. On my way in from the street corner I tried to think of the reality of twelve years. Twelve years ago you went to Paris for a week and didn't come back for months. In the course of twelve years your mother died; I got fired; we lost all our money in the crash; I had the accident. You went through a depression. In twelve years we went all the way into the abyss several times and pulled each other back."

He pushed the elevator button again. "Being twelve years late sounds romantic. Enigmatic. The kind of thing some of us might say at a gathering of pseudo-creative original writers. 'He was twelve years late to a meeting' could be a provocative opening line."

She looked at him, his eyes intense, his forehead wrinkled. One deep crease for each crisis.

"I'm sure Oliver didn't mean it that flippantly."

"I'm sure you're right."

The elevator arrived on the first floor. "Do you think it's safe to take it?" he asked. Then he handed her his umbrella. "If you have to go to the drugstore in the middle of the storm, at least use my umbrella. Otherwise you'll get drenched."

He got in the elevator and smiled at her through the glass as the elevator went slowly up.

She walked to the exit, opened Ben's umbrella, and stood outside. The storm was beginning to lose its fury, the heavy rain becoming a soothing drizzle. She could feel her limbs again. Oliver had surely left the corner after his encounter with Ben. She could call to tell him she was coming. Or she could stand there a few minutes longer, walk up the stairs to the fourth floor as if it were a day like any other. She thought of Oliver's first poem: "I saw a leaf at the bottom of the hill." She was that leaf, waiting for the wind to lift her into the life that would follow, and all things unknown.

About the author:

Israela Margalit is a critically-acclaimed playwright, television writer, concert pianist, recording artist, and recently a published author of short fiction and creative nonfiction, with awards or honors in all categories, including a Gold Medal, the New York Film & TV Festival, an Emmy Nomination, and Best CD the British Music Industry Awards. Her short stories have been published in anthologies and online in both British and American magazines.

Her story "California King Size" was a top 25-out of a 1000 Finalist at the Glimmer Train Press Very Short Story Competition. Her story "Too Much" was a Runnerup at the R. H. Cunningham Short Story Competition. Her story "A Whorehouse in Munich" was Nominated to Pen Short Story Prize for Emerging Writers. http://www.israelamargalit.com.

A BOY IN THE WOODS
©2018 by Carl Wooton

A small boy walked along a path deep in the thick woods that bordered a large lake. Bright sunshine filtered through the thick canopy of branches and leaves that made large areas of deep shade. The underbrush had not been cleared in years, and a thick layer of dead leaves covered the path. The boy shuffled his feet and kicked at the leaves and stirred up clouds of dust and the sharp odor of leaf mold and decay.

The boy was ten years old. He wore faded and dirty blue jeans and a polo shirt with broad, horizontal stripes. A cowlick made his straight brown hair fall constantly in his face. He had fine, almost delicate, features. He was thin, small-boned, with dark brown eyes that looked down or away whenever an adult asked him a question.

A man followed a few feet behind the boy. Every few steps the boy made quick glances over his shoulder. The man smiled when the boy turned to look at him. After they walked on for a few minutes, the boy noticed movement in a pile of leaves a few feet off the path. He stopped and held up his hand to motion for the man to stand still.

The man asked, "What's the matter?"

The boy put a finger to his lips and pointed at a squirrel sitting up on its haunches in the leaves.

The man said, "It's just a squirrel," and started to urge the boy to go on.

The boy said, "Don't move."

The man obeyed. The boy took a deep breath. The squirrel cocked its head and looked straight at the boy. The boy picked up his foot in slow motion and took a step toward the squirrel. He inhaled again, and when he lifted his foot, the squirrel turned and darted up a large tree. It stopped on the trunk, high enough to be out of reach and turned its head almost completely around. Then it climbed a couple of feet higher and looked again toward the boy before it disappeared in a thickness of branches and leaves. The boy wanted to climb the tree after the squirrel.

The man put a hand on the boy's shoulder and said, "Come on."

"Wait."

"You won't catch it."

The man turned the boy and pushed on his back. "Come on. My car's just a little ways up the path. I told you I would take you home."

The man put his arm around the boy's shoulders and pulled him close to his side. The boy pulled back and the man laughed and released him.

The boy asked, "What time is it?"

"Almost four."

The boy looked at him, disbelieving. The man showed him his watch and added, "I wouldn't lie to you."

"I have to get home before my father does."

His father had told him to stay out of the woods. He had told the boy a story about a child's body being found in the woods, all covered up with dry, brown leaves and fallen branches. Terrible things had happened to the boy, he had said, too terrible to explain what they were. He had told the story as though it was something that happened recently, but the boy thought it had to have been a long time ago, because he did not remember its happening.

The boy said, "I have to hurry."

"Then leave the squirrels alone."

The man pushed lightly on the boy's back between his shoulder blades and urged him to walk on. They came to a fork in the path and the man used only a slight pressure to turn the boy down the one that went to the left, away from the lake. In a few minutes, the boy saw the man's car, a black Ford coupe, standing in a small clearing.

"Race you," the man said and started to run, grabbing the boy's arm to pull him along. The boy tripped on a tree root and fell. His hip landed on a piece of broken limb hidden under the leaves. He cried out, and the man turned to help him up.

"Are you all right?"

"I'm fine." He fought back tears.

"Sure you are."

The man led the boy toward the car and opened the passenger side door. "I better look at that."

"It's all right."

"You might have cut yourself."

"I didn't."

The man smiled. "I better make sure."

The man bent forward and reached for the buckle on the boy's belt. He easily overcame the weak resistance of the boy's hands pushing against him. He undid the belt and worked the jeans and undershorts down to the boy's knees and put his hand on the boy's hip.

"It's not cut," the man said and moved his hand around to touch the boy's genitals. "It's getting big. You must be playing with it."

The boy blurted, "No I'm not."

The boy looked down at himself and wondered if the man could really tell that sometimes he played with himself. The man laughed, reached up, and mussed the boy's hair.

The boy reached down to pull up his jeans. The man stopped him, stood him up and turned him toward the car until the boy lay bent over with his face against the seat cushion. The boy tried to stand, but the man pressed his hand against the boy's back between his shoulder blades and held him firmly against the seat.

"Hold still," the man said.

Branches and leaves deflected sunlight through the windshield, and dust motes pirouetted in the bright air. The smells of dust, of stirred leaves, of dead wood, of stagnant water from the lake, tickled and burned the boy's nostrils. Sunlight and flickering shadows of leaves filled the space in front of his eyes, and the rough texture of the seat upholstery scratched his face. He felt some weight on his back, and a sharp pain cut through him, like a knife running up his spine to the base of his skull. He gasped for air, and his hands clawed the seat cushions.

In a moment the pain became something dull that pushed his face harder into the seat. The weight on his back got heavier, and the car moved beneath him, first slow, then faster, rhythmic like his rapid heart, like the dusty breath of the woods filling his lungs until he was sure they would burst.

He closed his eyes and made himself rise up through the roof of the car, beyond the trees, beyond the bright sky, past the clouds, past the sun, into a whirling darkness that was so deep it had to be the place where the silence of the woods came from. The darkness had a heart, and he felt it beating. He could neither see it nor hear it, but he felt it. It was not his heart, but it felt like it could have been. Then the car stopped moving, and the weight lifted itself off him.

"Stand up."

The man pulled on the boy's shoulder and helped him stand. He held out a rag to the boy. "Go over there in the bushes and take a dump. Use this to wipe yourself."

The boy took the rag and hobbled with his jeans and shorts pulled halfway up his legs. Something sticky wet the crack between his buttocks.

"Hurry up. I want to get you home before your daddy gets there. I wouldn't want you to get in trouble."

The boy did not speak during the ride home. When the man reached over and patted his knee, he squirmed and pulled himself as tightly against the door as he could.

The man said, in a comfortable, offhand way, "You know you

can't tell anyone, don't you?"

The boy did not answer.

"Don't you?"

The man's voice for the first time sounded menacing. "Something really bad might happen if you tell anyone. It would be sad if your father got hurt real bad some way because you told a story nobody would believe. You understand, don't you?"

The boy nodded and leaned his head out the window and let the wind strike him full in the face. The wind made his eyes burn, but he kept his face turned out to catch the wind until the car stopped in front of his house.

When the man stopped the car, he put his hand in his pocket and pulled out a quarter and tried to hand it to the boy.

"Here. Take it."

The boy looked at the coin held in the man's fingers and shook his head.

"Take it."

"No."

The man looked up at the house and saw the boy's sister, older by two years, sitting in the porch swing. He put the coin back in his pocket.

The boy said, "I have to go."

"You know you can't tell, don't you? I mean nobody. You understand that? Nobody."

"Yes."

The man made a fist and lightly punched the boy's arm. "Good boy."

The boy got out of the car and ran up to the front porch.

His sister said, "Don't worry. Daddy's not home yet. You're safe."

The clock on the wall over the kitchen stove said it was just after five. His mother moved about the kitchen preparing supper and nearly bumped into him with a pot of hot food she had just lifted off the stove.

"Supper won't be ready until your father gets home. Go do something until I call you."

As he turned to go, she said, "Wait."

She put the pot back on the stove, then reached and pulled at something in his hair. She handed him a piece of a leaf.

"Where did this come from?"

"I fell. In the back yard."

Even such a small lie made his face redden. He looked at his feet. If his mother noticed, she didn't say anything. She just held out the leaf for him to take.

"Throw this in the trash or take it outside. I don't need to be sweeping up dead leaves in my kitchen. Go on."

He went out into the back yard and tossed the leaf into the air so he could see which way the wind was blowing. It was something he had seen Tonto do in a movie. There was no wind. The leaf spun slowly to the ground, and he put his shoe on it and ground it until all that was left was dust.

The yard was small, not big enough for playing any kind of game. An old green apple tree grew near the back fence. The apples were not good for eating raw—cooking apples his mother called them—but the tree had low branches that made for easy climbing. He pulled himself up and climbed well up into the tree. The foliage was thick and the green apples were only beginning to fall. He liked sitting in the shadows of the leaves and branches and watching his mother through the kitchen window.

A sound turned him to look toward the elm tree that had thick dark branches up high, hanging over the roof of the house. A blur of brown leapt from the elm onto the roof and somehow came off the eave, turned itself upside down and disappeared into an air vent. His father was supposed to have repaired the screens on those vents weeks before to keep the squirrels from getting into the attic. If his mother heard the squirrel in the attic she would start fussing at his father until he promised again to get that hole stopped up, even though he knew it wouldn't do any good. Nobody could keep that squirrel out of anywhere it wanted to go.

After a while his mother called the boy in for supper. His father and sister were already seated at the table. His mother waited for the boy to get seated. Then she sat and bowed her head. Anyone looking through a window might have admired the scene: the family of four, their heads bowed at grace, a small bouquet of cut flowers in the center of the table. It could have been the perfect subject for a Norman Rockwell cover on *The Saturday Evening Post*.

His father asked the boy, "What did you do today?"

"Nothing."

"Where did you do it?"

"Out by the lake."

The boy choked on his own words. He hadn't meant to tell his father he had gone to the lake, but his father only looked at him, then smiled.

"I thought your bike has a flat tire."

"I walked."

"That's a good ways to walk, hot as it is."

Depending on which part of town one lived in, the farthest distance to the lake was a little more than a mile and a half, and it was not uncommon back then, in that safer time, for boys to walk to it.

"How did you get home?"

The boy swallowed hard, took a drink from the glass of milk by his plate, and looked down at his hands in his lap.

"How did you get home?"

The boy was afraid to say who had brought him home, afraid his father might guess something about him being with the man. He looked at his sister. She had seen him come home in the man's car, and the boy didn't know whether she would blurt it out if he didn't tell.

He said, "I got a ride," and he stopped.

His father waited a moment, then asked, "Who with?"

The boy told him, and his father looked at the mother and again at the boy for a long moment before he said, "Don't go getting into cars with anyone we don't know."

The boy knew his father had met the man at a burial service for a local man, a Marine who had been killed on some island in the Pacific. The man had shown up in his navy uniform to help carry the casket. After the funeral, the boy's father had lined up with other men of the town to shake hands with the pallbearers and to thank them for being so upstanding. His father had said the pallbearers were all good men because they had fought in the war.

His mother said, "I baked a pie. Anybody want some?"

Without waiting for an answer, she got up and went into the kitchen.

The boy's father said, "Did you go into the woods?"

"Just a little ways."

He didn't hesitate to answer. He had already given up the fact that he had gone to the lake, and anybody would know that it was almost impossible to go to the lake without going at least a little way into the woods.

"You remember what I told you about that, don't you?"

"Yes, sir."

"You're not old enough to remember, but a child got murdered in there once."

The boy couldn't think of a way to respond to his father's remark. He didn't want to tell his father he had begun to wonder if it was true. He had asked friends at school about the story, but none of them could remember a child being murdered in the woods.

He became uncomfortable in the silence, and if only to hear his own voice, he said, "I almost caught a squirrel."

His mother came into the room with the pie and plates and set them on the table.

She said, "You leave those animals alone. Some of them have rabies."

His sister said, "He thinks he's a squirrel. He's always up in that tree. Looks like one, too."

Before he could answer back, his mother said, "Stop it," and glared the boy and his sister into silence. Then she turned to the father.

"Since we're on the subject. When exactly are you going to plug up that hole I told you about? The sound of those squirrels running back and forth in the attic woke me up at three o'clock this morning."

His father said, "Saturday."

"That's what you said last week."

"Dammit, I'll do it *this* Saturday."

That exchange between his parents took away any attention being paid to the boy, and he used the opportunity to finish his dessert and ask to be excused from the table.

Gray twilight spread through the summer night sky. He went out and looked for Venus. He knew it was always the first star to be seen at night. His teacher had told him it wasn't really a star; it was a planet. He liked finding it in the evening, but he almost never got up early enough to see it in the morning.

As the sky darkened he chased fireflies and put them in a glass jar with a lid he had punched holes in to let the fireflies have air. He always let them go. He played hide-and-go-seek with a half-dozen other kids from the neighborhood. He had become really clever at hiding. He was almost always the last one to be found. Sometimes he would stay hidden until the others were forced to give up and quit the game. And sometimes he kept himself hidden away until his mother came out on the porch and called for him to come in. He could not have told anyone why, but those were the best nights.

After his bath, his parents allowed him to go to his room and read for another half hour while they stayed in the living room and listened to the radio. He read a story about Frank Merriwell, the most extraordinary athlete in every sport he had ever heard of. The boy was, in fact, an avid reader, a trait that more than a few times had often prompted his father to ask if it was healthy for him to read so much. A teacher asked the class once what their parents read at home, and it hurt him to answer he didn't think they read anything, except maybe the Sunday newspaper.

He heard the radio go silent, and he knew what was coming next. His mother came into the room, waited for him to finish the page and took the book and laid it on a shelf on the other side of the room.

She said, "It's bedtime. Get ready. I'll come back in a little bit," and as she left the room, she added, "Don't forget to brush your teeth."

He undressed and put on his pajamas in the bathroom. He didn't forget to brush his teeth, but he avoided looking in the mirror over the sink because he was afraid he might see a mark on his skin, or an unnatural speck in the color of his eyes, a sign that would tell the world the secret he was never to tell anyone, never, not ever, if he didn't want his father to get hurt. His boy mind thought that if he didn't look, it wouldn't be there, but if he looked, and he saw it, then, he believed, everyone could see it.

When he had been in the bed a few minutes, his mother returned, and he watched her as she came near the bed. He didn't need even the thin sheet he had pulled up over him, but he clung tightly to its edge in a way that would make it easy for him to pull it over his head in case she leaned over to kiss him. She acted as though she didn't notice. Earlier that same summer, she had stopped kissing him goodnight after several instances of him obviously turning away, trying to avoid the kiss. She thought he was acting out his little boy's skewed perception of maleness.

Truth was, tonight he feared if she came too close to him, if she touched him with her lips, or if he let her look too close in his eyes, she might know. She often confounded him by knowing what he had done, where he had been, what he had said when he believed it wasn't possible. At times, he thought she knew *everything*, and the fear squeezed his chest until he had to gasp for a breath. That fear multiplied itself like stars growing in the sky when she turned out his light.

As she closed his door, she said, "Sweet dreams."

He lay in the dark and listened to the soft sounds the house made at night. He could barely hear music from the radio in his parents' bedroom and the soft murmur of their voices. He looked at the ceiling and thought he heard the rapid patter of the squirrels running in the attic. He wished he had x-ray vision so he could see through the ceiling and the dark. He wished he could live with them in the attic, and he fell asleep thinking about the squirrels.

He dreamt about being in the woods by himself and he was frightened. He seemed alone, but he knew someone was looking for him. He followed one path after another, constantly turning his head and looking over his shoulder. Every few steps he stopped and listened, but he heard absolutely nothing. Here and there he caught movement in the corner of his eye, but when he turned toward it, he saw only the woods: thick, heavy trees and deep underbrush, and the acrid smell of dust and mildew and rot.

He went on until he came into a large clearing. Squirrels chattered in a tree above him. Leaves rustled with the movement of squirrels running along the branches. A brown head popped out and disappeared. A brown tail stuck through the leaves. Small, beady eyes, then more eyes and more eyes all the time, glistened in the tiny spaces between leaves as high up as he could see.

A large fallen tree lay across the clearing, and he sat on it so that he looked directly at the hugest tree he had ever seen. As soon as he sat, a squirrel ran down the trunk of the tree, headed straight for a pile of dead leaves, stopped, looked around, then pushed its head into the leaves and came back out with something in its mouth. It sat up and looked around again, this way and that way, the way the boy sometimes did when he wanted to sneak past an open door that led to a room full of adults.

The boy held himself perfectly still. The squirrel ran a few feet back toward the big tree, stopped, swiveled its head to look around the clearing and looked straight at the boy. Both the boy and the squirrel held their breath, and the boy felt the squirrel's eyes lock onto his.

What did it know? What did it see? Was there something he couldn't see but was visible to others? Was there something about the way he walked? Would older boys make jokes about him being bowlegged, saying his legs were pleasure bent, the way they said it about some girls.

Another squirrel came down the tree, then another and another, until brown and gray squirrels filled the clearing. Each one seemed to take its turn to run in front of the boy, stop, look at him, nod its head, and yield its place to yet another squirrel. This went on until all the squirrels had taken their turn. Then they ran in a steady flow of five, six, or seven at a time, up the big tree to hide in all the branches and leaves.

The last two squirrels stopped halfway up the trunk and looked back at the boy. One of them waved its tail excitedly and chattered in a way that made the boy think it was asking him to come closer.

A man's voice shouted somewhere in the woods, and the boy jumped up and ran toward the tree. The pair of squirrels moved down toward him but stayed half an arm's length out of reach. They started a rapid chatter, then ran up the tree a way, stopped, looked back at the boy, chattered some more, and ran up a little farther. He stepped closer to the tree, stretched his arms upward, and felt himself being lifted into the canopy of the leaves and branches of the tree, and he understood the chattering choir telling him, *Hide, little squirrel, hide.*

When the boy woke, sweat had made his pajamas stick to his skin. The images of the dream clung to his mind, as though they were right behind his eyes, and it took him a few seconds to realize just where he was. Gray light seeped through the blind on his bedroom window, and he watched it slowly brighten. He heard the sounds of others moving around, the sound of water flowing from a tap, and his parents' radio being turned up. He tried hard to hold on to the last fragments of the dream. For a moment—hardly that—it seemed he heard the chatter of the squirrels, but it all disappeared when his mother stuck her head in the room and told him to get up and get dressed.

He got up, took off his pajamas, put on clean underwear and pants and shirt and socks and shoes. He went into the bathroom, relieved himself, and brushed his teeth, avoiding the mirror. Then he went to the kitchen where his parents sat drinking coffee at the table.

His father said, "Looks like you're ready for another day."

His mother said, "Did you make your bed?"

His father said, "Remember what I said about those woods. You stay out of there."

"Yes, sir."

His mother said, "The bed."

After he made his bed and ate a bowl of cereal, and after his father had gone to work and while his mother gathered clothes to put in the wash, he went outside and climbed the apple tree and watched for the squirrels to come out of the attic vent and jump onto the long, dark branch of the elm.

The boy sat in the tree and felt the day get warmer, felt the weight of muggy air, and watched for the squirrels. Quick, brown movement caught his eye and he saw a squirrel come from the vent. The squirrel did its upside-down trick to get onto the roof and run for the elm tree. The boy watched it leap onto the branch, then leap again onto a lower branch and disappear in the foliage. A second one followed, and the boy could hear them chattering, invisible behind the leaves. He closed his eyes and strained to understand what the squirrels might be saying. He wished he could climb higher in the apple tree and leap the wide distance to the larger elm. He wanted, more than he would ever want anything else in his whole life, to be a squirrel and to live safely hidden by the leaves of the elm forever.

About the author:

Carl Wooton has been writing and teaching for more than fifty years. His fiction, poetry, and essays have appeared in a variety of journals and literary reviews. His fiction is in *The Hudson Review* (four stories), *Literary Review, Blue Lake Review, Green Briar Review, Sun Dog, Forum*, Ball State University *Forum, Cayuhoga Review, Georgia Review, Crow's Nest, Slackwater Review, Revue de Louisiane, Laurel Review, Beloit Fiction Journal, Ellery Queen's Mystery Magazine, Chatauqua Literary Review,* and in the anthology *Rigorous Mortis* and other journals. In 1990, he co-authored *Ernest Gaines: Conversations on the Writer's Craft,* with Marcia Gaudet (LSU Press). He retired first in 1993, after teaching for twenty-eight years at University of Louisiana-Lafayette. Not even moving to California's coast could make him not want to return to the classroom. He taught twenty more years at Cal Poly State University in San Luis Obispo until June, 2013. At 83 years old, he still writes and is working on two novellas, a collection (maybe two) of stories, and a novel in whatever amount of energy and time he is allowed. To paraphrase (badly) Achilles, Life is hard, but any part of it is a damned sight better than the alternative.

He has seven sons/stepsons, twelve grandchildren, two great grandchildren. He lives with his wife, Dolores, in Nipomo, California.

SHE WHO MADE THE LAND HER HOME
©2018 by Stephen Matlock

The flames leapt from the stone circle, consuming the sticks and branches atop glowing coals. Sparks danced through smoke and fire, spiraling into the dark sky.

"Tell us a story, Auntie!"

"Yes, tell us a story!"

Auntie Danquah beamed at the children around her, the children of Tafuaa, a village twelve dozen kilometers from Accra. So young, so happy, so clever they were! Gaddo was just that day reprimanded for painting his dog with spectacles, while Akosua, busy at schoolwork, laughed out loud and woke Auntie Danquah from her morning nap. Akosua would be a doctor someday for the Ghanaian Health Administration, and Gaddo would surely be her first patient when he came in bloodied from his saucy mouth.

"Oh children, it is late and your beds await you. Even now your *Ene* and *Agya*, your mothers and fathers, prepare for your night sleep with water to wash in and fresh clothes for slumber." She glanced at lights flickering on, one by one, as families prepared for the evening's rest before tomorrow's work.

A childless widow, Auntie Danquah had no formal job and only a room in the house of her niece. In life she was not idle, and in age she did not cease her work. She was the village elder and story-spinner, watching their children before their beds, casting shadows in the dark to educate and enchant.

"Oh, Nyaméama, sitting there alone in the dark. I see you. What story would you want? One of panthers and hunters? Of gold and adventure?"

Nyaméama Amoateng was silent. She was the youngest, left out of games, as she was born little. Her very name meant "little"—names were important in Ghana. They told everyone your family and your meaning, even if you were a surprise or unfavored.

Nyaméama looked down at her bare feet and twisted a leaf in her hand. "I would like to hear of Mother Sowah, the hero of Ghana. The story where she runs like wind through grass, flows like water through stones, burns through forests like flames, and sparkles like fire in the dark, dark night," she whispered.

Auntie rocked back and opened her eyes wide. "You are a wise child. You have remembered a story from long ago."

Auntie looked at the other children around the fire, hearing the crackle of burning wood and the chittering of animals in the dark. The glowing brown faces with wide eyes told her to continue.

"All right, children, draw near and I shall tell you the story of the orphan Kaakyire, who lost her family and home, saved our nation, and found again her new home.

"It was long, long ago, so long ago that the Three Rivers of Ghana flooded strong under the stars, no dam or bridge to block the waters. The forests were somber, with the people living in strife and fear, building strong walls and tall fences, shutting out others in their unhappiness.

"But some hoped for better, for themselves, their families, and even their villages. Of them all, in the village of Tafuaa—"

"That's right here! That's our village!" A young girl leapt to her feet, her eyes wide and her mouth open.

"Hush. The story will tell all, if you listen.

"Now, in the family of Sowah, there was a little girl, Kaakyire, last in her family, but beloved of her father Kwaw and his wife Mensah. Strong in heart, small in frame, she gathered wood for the *mukiya* clay oven, drew the water for bathing and cooking, and swept the compound of her family of four sisters and five brothers, not to mention that of her mother's brother, Ataá Kúmaa Kyekyeku, with his own wife, Máanu, and his six children."

Komla interrupted. "Her oldest brother was Bekoe the hunter!" He sat down, happy to add to the story.

"Yes, Bekoe Sowah was a mighty hunter, as were all her brothers, and all her sisters were dutiful. But Kaakyire had a secret. If she did her work quickly, she could spend time reading and learning about her village and her land. Who can tell me how she found that time? Nkroma? Was it in doing poor work, or refusing the requests of her mother, or disobeying her father?"

"No!" she shouted. "She began to run everywhere, from task to task, chore to chore. From well to wood to water, she ran and ran, faster and faster, until she could run for miles without a stop for breath or a drink of water."

The children grew quiet. They knew the next part.

"Yes. She ran. But then the invaders came. They came one day when Kaakyire was running through fields and forests. When she returned, the village was empty, with homes smoking piles of rubble.

"Kaakyire cried at the sight. Her family and village was destroyed; only a lucky accident had kept her away."

A small girl next to Akosua grabbed her arm and turned her head into Akosua's shoulder.

"Kaakyire was left without family, without home, without anyone to remember her. But she knew that her father came from Kpenfa to the north, her aunt came from Kibiye to the east, her mother came from Abosani to the west, and she, herself, was born in Tafuaa.

That very day, she would go to the lands of her family for the restoration of her village. That very day, she would not stop running until her village, her land, even all the people were united as one, against invaders and for each other. That very day, she called herself Okwan Sowah, the one found on the road.

"So she ran and ran all the night, miles and miles, until she came to Kpenfa, anxious and expectant from running. It was morning and the village was arising from their sleep.

"'Who are you, child, and why are you running?' they asked her. 'My father, Kwaw, is from here,' she replied. 'We lived in Tafuaa until the invaders came. I have no family or home, and I seek your help.'

"Now the villagers were suspicious of an orphan. Without a father or mother, aunt or uncle, who was this child, then? Was she rightfully lost or only a young girl running away?

"She told them of her life and family, of how she worked hard, how she was obedient, how she dreamed one day to lead her people.

"'You are a good child of your father and mother, aunt and uncle, sister and brother, cousin and cousin,' Kumi the warrior said. 'We can give weapons to fight against the invader. They cannot bring back your family or rebuild your village, but they can defend you and all you love. They are red with blood for valor and defense.'"

Gaddo leapt up. "And weapons for killing! Pow pow! Skree! Niauuuuuuh!" he shouted.

Auntie shook her head. "Yes, weapons can kill, but a wise man knows that sometimes a pinprick is better than broken bones. And Kaakyire was wise, even wiser than wisest of men. 'I will return when I have restored the village,' she said.

"She picked up the weapons, but they were heavy. The villagers saw her burden and said 'We will bring your weapons to Tafuaa.'

"She ran now to Kibiye in the east, where her mother's sister was from. She ran all day until night was falling and entered the village. It was dry and dusty, and busy with people closing up shops and pulling down screens. Kibiye was a market town, with many businesses and many people buying and selling, shouting and laughing. They saw her and stopped to stare at her, dusty from running.

"'Who are you, child, and why are you running?' they asked her. 'My mother's sister Máanu is from here. We lived in Tafuaa until the invaders came. I have no family and no home, and I seek your help,' she said.

"'What would you have us do? We are busy with buying and selling, with profit and banks and storerooms. We cannot help you in running. We cannot help you in fighting,' they said.

"Kaakyire was downcast, and said, as quiet as embers slumbering to ashes, 'I have weapons from Kpenfa but no one to fight.'

"The villagers nodded. 'We understand. We cannot fight, as we are merchants, but we know in our wisdom that one can buy the arm of a warrior. Here, here is our yellow gold and white silver, coins and jewels, emeralds and amber and rubies. Take these and buy warriors,' Afiriyie the merchant said.

"And they gave her gold, silver, and jewels, so much that their heaviness bowed her in pain.

"The villagers saw her burden and said 'We will bring your gold and jewels to Tafuaa.'

"Now it was night again, and she set off to the west, to run until morning. The sun was rising over the smoking lake water when she came to Abosani. A farmer emerged from his shack, rubbing his eyes and yawning, going to the corral where goats and chickens were awakening at the first rays of sun. Other villagers soon rose to attend to their duties. And they saw Kaakyire, pale with sweat from running.

"'What do you want, child, and why are you so worried? Are you not tired? Are your mother and father so cruel as to give you tasks at night as well as day?' they asked.

"'My mother, Mensah, is from here. We lived in Tafuaa until the invaders came. I have no family and no home, and I seek your help. My uncle and aunt and all my cousins, along with my family and my village, were taken in the night by invaders. I have weapons, and gold and jewels to hire an army, and I seek your help,' she said.

"'We have no weapons or armies here. We are a peaceful farming and fishing village. We can offer only food and drink for the day.'

"Kaakyire was sad. 'I will fail, then, for weapons are dull without warriors, and warriors are weak without food.'

"Afúom the farmer looked at her and bowed. 'We can offer food for your army. We have goats and chickens from green pastures. We have fish from the river, plantains and yams and cassava from green farms. With these you can feed the warriors who will fight the invaders, and who will bring back your family,' he said.

"They piled a basket high with goods and lay it on her shoulders.

"She looked at them and was sad. 'I cannot carry so much for the warriors.'

"The villagers saw her burden and said 'We will bring your meats and your vegetables and your fruits to Tafuaa.'"

A young boy fidgeted, then swatted a night insect, scowling. "It bit me!"

"Hush. The story is half over and soon done." Auntie turned to the boy. "Can you tell me where she ran next?"

"She ran back home to Tafuaa! And then she met—"

Auntie put her hand over his mouth. "Answer one question with one answer. It is better and wiser to stay on the branch near the tree rather than venture out to the tip where you will fall off."

Several children giggled at this wise saying.

"Now then, let us continue. Yes, she did run back to Tafuaa where she would see the red weapons and golden coins and the food from green farms. She stood in the empty village. 'I am so sleepy and aching that I will rest for a week,' she said. But she did not rest for a week or even a night. She was awakened at dawn by the sounds of feet shuffling on dusty ground, the clinking of sharp weapons, the soft bleating of goats and the clucking of chickens.

"'What has happened?' she said, rising up and stretching. The sun blinded her with yellow and green and red sparks. "She opened her eyes, awake now. As far as she could see there were warriors with their weapons, sharp and glinting in the sun, warriors from the east and north and west. There were gold coins and jewels around their necks and arms. There were roasting goats and chickens, and mats with yams and plantains and cassava laid out, with men feasting and boasting, ready to stand and fight."

"I know how it ends!" shouted another young boy.

Auntie laughed, too. "Yes, we know how it ends. Kaakyire led the warriors into battle. They were strong and proud and tall, and they drove out the invaders, and restored the land."

"But what happened next is the most extraordinary thing, a thing you would not imagine in a lifetime of imaginings. 'You have brought us all together by running from village to village, not for gifts but for help for others, one village to another. We have talked the talks in the night, and we have seen the strength we have when we stand together,' they said. 'We will be one nation now, and you will be our leader, a woman who has tied our land together and made us safe in our homes. And we will no longer call you Kaakyire Last Born. We will no longer call you Okwan Path Runner. We will call you Ntonni, the Hero of our land.'

"'But I have no home,' she said. 'My home is burned and my family gone.'

"'Your home is always with us, wherever you may go, however far you may run,' they said."

The children were at once anxious and happy, for the end of the story was near.

"Then they said, 'We have a sign now for our land, where red and gold and green come together, the far lands and the close lands to make one land.'

"And she said, 'But what of my family? What do I bring of myself?'"

Then Auntie brought out an old book from long ago. She flipped to a well-worn spot to show them a familiar sight. "What do you see here?"

"The flag of Ghana!"

"And what do the colors of the flag represent?"

"Red for courage and blood, gold for prosperity and light, and green for fields and land and food," replied Nyaméama, the littlest one.

"And what is in the center?" she asked.

Nyaméama broke out in a wide, wide smile. "The black star of Africa, the star of Ntonni, the star of all people who make the land of Ghana great."

Auntie Danquah closed the book. The fire had died down to low coals hidden among gray ashes. "Now off to bed with you. Be sure you wash and dress, say your prayers, and dream good dreams."

She watched them scamper away, where their fathers and mothers stood in the lights of their homes, and she smiled.

And Auntie Kaakyire Okwan Ntonni Danquah-Sowah, Mother of Ghana, leaned back, rubbing her legs and feet, still sore from the many years gone of running for family, for home, and for Ghana.

About the author:

Stephen J. Matlock is a full-time writer and a part-time author and gardener, often overwhelmed by both words and weeds. Along the way to adulthood (a promised destination and not a requirement of the journey) he has tried his hand at many things, from running a restaurant to working at Crate Expectations (a mill for building shipping containers), and even technical writing, where the goal is to tell people what to do, but nicely. He lives with his wife in the Pacific Northwest and has seen his children fly away to build their own lives, although they do return regularly for food, advice, and help on finding what that pesky sound in the car engine means other than money. He is a member of the Christian & Missionary Alliance, and like most people in his faith community, is still working out the details of what it means to follow Jesus.

www.ingramcontent.com/pod-product-compliance
Lightning Source LLC
Chambersburg PA
CBHW051256170626
46809CB00004B/1669